Caster & Fleet 1

The
Case
of the
Black
Tulips

Paula Harmon
Liz Hedgecock

WHITE
RHINO
BOOKS

ISBN-13: 978-1983280979

For Millicent Fawcett

CHAPTER 1
Katherine

The house had felt lost at sea for two days. Yellow fog pressed against the windows and seeped under the outer doors. On Saturday afternoon, when I came home from work, I could barely breathe and stood gasping on the doormat, trying to replace the sulphurous tar with the smell of baking. Once inside, I felt as if my household were the only people in the world. Outside, wheels and steps were muffled, street-lights indistinct. Anything near the window frames was, despite Ada's best efforts, smeared in oily dirt. Even Aunt Alice, unable to face the London fog, hadn't insisted on church on Sunday.

It was almost a relief to wake to pouring rain on Monday morning.

Almost. I stood in the hall and wrestled Father's umbrella from the stand. It was two-thirds my height; unfurled it would be twice my width. I would be a menace,

1

beetling along as I forged my way through other pedestrians. A fresh gust battered the door. I looked down at my feet in their thin shoes, and the hem of my nicest office skirt.

'There's nothing for it, Katherine,' said Aunt Alice. 'You'll have to wear galoshes and your father's raincoat.'

Father is six feet tall. I am four foot ten. I would look utterly ridiculous. I felt my shoulders sag as I buttoned the galoshes and eyed his old-fashioned raincoat. I weighed up the options; I could be drenched but stylish, or stay dry and resemble a walking advertisement for second-hand clothes.

Aunt Alice shook her head. 'There's no point in wearing good things in this deluge without a coat. By the time you arrive they will be ruined. You won't attract a nice young man that way.'

'I'm not interested in attracting a nice young man,' I said.

'Well then, there's no reason not to put on the coat. Although perhaps…' She paused as a fresh onslaught of water crashed against the door. 'Perhaps you could take a cab.'

'We can't afford a cab. The omnibus will be fine.'

Aunt Alice said nothing. Her lips thinned, then she said, as she always did on Mondays, 'I do think your father could have left things better organised when he went away. I don't hold with women working.'

As usual, I nodded towards the kitchen where our maid Ada washed the breakfast dishes before starting the laundry, then pointed discreetly up the stairs as our lodger Miss Robson descended, dressed for her secretarial job. Aunt Alice waggled her head as if to say 'yes but they're different', and helped me on with the coat.

'Could you not share a cab?' she asked.

'That's a kind thought,' said Miss Robson, 'but we're going in different directions.'

Aunt Alice tutted.

Opening the door, I was nearly blinded by the wind-driven rain. A bedraggled shape clumped up the steps and rummaged in a bag.

'First post, Miss,' said the postman, handing over a letter which became sodden and smudged in the seconds it took to change hands. I glanced at the smearing ink.

R Demeray Esq., 7 Mulberry Avenue, Fulham.

'Is it for me?' said Miss Robson, buttoning her neat mackintosh.

'No.'

She sighed, but I couldn't tell whether she was responding to my answer or the weather. Before I could say goodbye, she opened her umbrella, marched down the steps into the street and turned the corner.

'I'll take it,' said Aunt Alice, sheltering behind the door.

'No. It's...' I shoved the letter into my bag and wrestled the umbrella open. 'I'll take it with me.'

A few minutes later I was sitting on the omnibus dripping. It was, as I'd told Aunt Alice, fine. That is, as a means of getting to the office. Otherwise it was revolting. Water from coats and umbrellas ran along the floor. The windows were steamed with breath and the air full of tobacco smoke. The odour brought to mind wet old dogs carrying long-dead rats which they'd fished from the muddy armpit of an inveterate smoker. Fog would almost have been preferable.

I heaved my arm free from a stout, perspiring man with

a pipe, and pulled the letter from my bag. The envelope was good quality and despite its drenching did not open easily. There were smudgy ink marks on the front and back. Inside was a short letter in an old-fashioned hand.

Dear Mr Demeray,

Please forgive my writing to you but I am so very afraid. I have tried to send for help but I ~~am told~~ fear I am imagining things or worse, mad. And indeed when I heard their voices plotting in the fog, I thought it was simply distortion of sound or my own nervousness playing tricks on my mind. They said someone called Mary was missing and I remembered that name, hissed in the swirling yellow beyond the lamps. It made me think of kindness but I can't recall why. And I thought they said the name Meg, although perhaps I'm mistaken.

Mr Demeray, is it true I wrote to you once before and asked for your help? Your name is famous of course, and perhaps I thought you could find something out for me. I feel that if I did it was because our families were once long ago acquainted, not simply because your books are full of the mysteries you find on your travels. Did you reply? I know you are fascinated by things which have no simple explanation. I do not know if this has a simple explanation or indeed what is afoot but I cannot shake off my fear. I am afraid your replies may have been intercepted or perhaps I am not where I think I am. Perhaps I am not even who I think I am. I do not know much of the world these days as I ~~am not all~~ do not venture outside anymore. But I am now so desperate for advice.

If you can help, please could you put a notice in the personal column in the Times with reference to black

4

tulips. That was what I'd asked you to find out about, I think. Please help. If somehow I receive your answer, I will write again. I am afraid for Mary and for myself.

   Yours
   An Admirer

'Isn't this your stop, Miss?' said the conductor.

The omnibus was coming to a halt. I shoved the letter into my bag and stood, wrenching my coat and skirt from under the stout man. He grunted at me and I caught his shin with my umbrella as I made my way down the aisle.

On the pavement I took a breath of wet but comparatively fresh air and looked up at The Department. In the rain, its grey Georgian right-angles seemed more supercilious than ever. Its windows were like the cold eyes of a monster, sneering at the small sodden woman climbing its wet dark steps and entering its maw through the heavy oak doors.

The letter seemed to burn through the leather of my bag. What had the writer expected Father to do? I needed time to think, but I would be locked in the office with a typewriter all day. A desperate woman had written to Father, but Father had been on his travels for three years without a word. Everyone said he must be dead. Then a thought crossed my mind: what if the writer wasn't the person who was in danger? After all, Mary and Meg are common names. My little sister's pet name is Meg. A chill went through me.

It was down to me to work out what to do. Only I didn't know where to start.

CHAPTER 2
Connie

It had been a thoroughly trying morning. Even for a Monday.

I had thought a trip into town would spare me from the worst of Mother's fussing; but submitting to a lecture at breakfast was the price of escape. 'Make sure you get something suitable,' she said, darkly. 'Nothing too modern. If you turn up at the Frobishers' dinner looking like a maypole I shall pretend I don't know you.'

'Well, if all the clothes budget wasn't being spent on Helena —'

'She's the debutante this year.' Mother's ice-blue gaze was sharp as a rapier. 'You had your turn three years ago, Constance, and not a proposal to show for it.'

'Mother!' I hissed, my eyes flicking to the parlourmaid smirking behind her chair.

'It's true. With Veronica to come out after Helena, we can't afford to be dressing you *a la mode*. Get thee to the ready-to-wear department.' She drained her coffee and stood, ramrod-straight. 'I should never have called you Constance, you're as changeable as the wind.'

'You're obviously a bad judge of character, Mother. Look at Jemima, she's the opposite of peaceful.'

'Your sister may be . . . peppery in her temperament, but she's marrying an Honourable.' Mother smiled as if she thought the title would cow me. As if I cared.

'If she doesn't roast Charles alive first. And as for Helena —' My sister Helena was sweet and placid, but dark, short, and rather broad. I could see why Mother was focusing on getting her dressed up for her debut.

'Now who's talking out of turn?' snapped my mother. 'Unlike you, Constance, I have things to do. This household won't run itself. I shall see you later.' And with that threat she swept out, the short train on her day dress slithering over the breakfast-room parquet.

I wiped the last piece of toast round my plate. 'Can someone ask Hodgkins to get the carriage out for ten o'clock?'

'I'm sorry, Miss Connie,' came the respectful reply. 'It's already promised to Miss Jemima.'

'Where's she going, Palmer?'

'I couldn't say, Miss.'

I sighed. 'I'll get a cab, then.' Our house, in the fashionable part of Pimlico, was a two-mile walk from the shops of Oxford and Regent Street, where I intended to begin my quest for a dress suitable for small-talk at the Frobishers'. In addition, the rain had poured down all morning, and I was in no mood to add a chill to my troubles.

'Very well, miss. I'll have one waiting.'

In retrospect, watching the world go about its business,

while I sped by in a cosy cab, shielded by glass and raindrops, was the best two minutes of the day. The rest of the morning was spent in various draper's shops, being measured, appraised, and generally sized up. And the verdict? 'Madame's figure is — a little ahead of its time,' sighed the petite French dressmaker. 'We have nothing in stock.'

'Couldn't you let the seams out on that green dress?'

She shook her head regretfully. 'There is — how you say — insufficient allowance.' She beamed at having got the words out. 'Madame is . . . is —'

'Don't say it.' I gritted my teeth.

'Say what, Madame?'

'Like a ship in full sail. No!' I held my hand up at her look of delighted comprehension. 'I've had enough of "stately" and "queenly" and all that rubbish. I'm just tall, and broad, and inconveniently sized, and no amount of corsetry can do anything about it. What am I going to do?'

She put her thin little hand on my shoulder. 'Perhaps Madame would care to consider something bespoke?'

I winced. 'I'll have to speak to my mother.'

It was the same story in every establishment. Nowhere had anything suitable ready-made that they could adjust to fit me. My stomach growled; but I could not face lunch at home, with Mother. She would ask, and I would have to tell her, and suffer the wrath of a perfectly-proportioned woman who simply cannot understand what the problem is. So I did what any sensible person would do and repaired to the nearest restaurant, assisted by a draper's boy with a large umbrella.

It was a restaurant I had never visited; and as soon as I stepped across the threshold, I felt out of place. It was a drab, cramped little room, despite its fashionable location, filled with a motley of people. Shoppers, office workers, even the occasional City gent, tucking into plates of brown stuff, slurping at tea or gulping beer, talking, reading newspapers, and generally taking up room. Their damp clothes steamed in the heat, and the whole place smelt of mildew, stale perfume, and gravy.

'You staying, miss?' said a waitress, whisking by.

I considered leaving, but I had no umbrella, and the draper's boy was long gone. I nodded, and she flapped a hand at a vacant seat nearby. I pulled out the chair, the scrape lost in the buzz around me, and sat down.

Sitting opposite was a young red-haired woman, perhaps my age or a little older, huddled over a plate of grey stew and reading a letter. I couldn't tell if the smudged writing on it was through rain or tear-stains.

She raised her eyes and noticed me looking at the blurred ink. She glared at me, then stuffed the letter into its equally-smudged envelope and put it into a pocket of the large man's coat slung on the back of her chair. 'Correspondence is generally presumed private,' she snapped. She picked up her cutlery and with something like a grimace started to eat.

Where was I supposed to look? 'I didn't mean to,' I said. 'Sorry.'

'Mmph.' She dissected a dumpling and inspected a beige fragment.

'Is it nice?'

She froze. 'Is what nice?'

'The, er, stew. I haven't been here before.'

'Oh.' She considered. 'It's edible. Just about.'

'Ah.' I consulted the menu and the waitress was at my

9

side in an instant. 'Can I have a pork chop, please, with mashed potatoes and green peas, and a cup of coffee.'

'Right away, ma'am.' The waitress bustled off and I stretched my legs out under the table.

'Ow!' The young woman's brows knitted together, and she reached down to rub her leg.

'Sorry,' I said again. 'There isn't much room.'

'No, there isn't. Which is why you're meant to keep your feet on your own side.'

'It's all right for you,' I muttered. 'You're small.'

'I've paid for my bit of the table,' she said. 'Size doesn't matter.'

'Tell that to the dressmakers,' I snorted. The waitress returned with my coffee. I took a sip and as I lowered the cup, caught her looking at me, eyebrows raised. 'If you must know, I've had a very frustrating morning.'

Her eyebrows climbed higher.

'I have to buy a dinner party dress,' I said, feeling defensive. 'All the clothes money has gone to my debutante sister, and nothing ready-made will fit. Mother'll have the vapours when I tell her.'

Her eyebrows returned to their usual place, and she put her cutlery down in the very middle of her plate. When she looked up, her eyes blazed green. 'I got drenched on the way to work this morning,' she said, very quietly. 'I have been typing letters for four hours already today, and when I return I shall have to type for another four. My fingers ache, and cramp, but I have to work to bring money into the house. And someone has written a strange letter to my missing father, asking for help. I'm afraid your party dress dilemma doesn't really interest me.' Her chair scraped back, and she flounced to the counter before I could reply,

10

the enormous coat slung over her arm.

'Your pork chop, ma'am.' The waitress set down a steaming plate, and as I looked at the glistening meat, the heap of mashed potato, and the bright green peas, I wondered how much more my meal had cost than the young woman's plate of dismal stew. Sometimes I had thought that having a career and being a young woman about town might be rather interesting; but typing for eight hours a day was not quite what I had had in mind. At any rate, Mother would never allow it. Conscience cleared, I made a hearty meal and called for the bill.

I collected my things, and as I rose to leave —

'Miss! Your letter!'

The clerk at the next table was pointing to a white rectangle on the floor.

'Oh no, that isn't my… Oh, how silly of me.'

'I'll get it,' he said, leaning down and swiping it from the ground. 'There.'

'Thank you so much.' I looked at the envelope in my gloved hand. *R Demeray, Esq.*, in a fine, slanting hand. It must have fallen from her pocket when she left.

The address was severely rain-blotted, but I made out a *7* after a splash, then *Mulber—y A—ue, Fulham.*

It wasn't an area I had ever been to.

Should I leave the letter at the counter? She might come back for it.

Or someone else might take it.

No, the proper thing to do was to return it. Anyway, I had already claimed it as mine. I put the letter into my bag, smiled at the clerk, and stepped into the street.

By some miracle the rain had stopped, and I strolled along. At least my own problem seemed much smaller in size, now that I had something to distract me. I must find Miss — I consulted the envelope — Demeray and give her the letter. I looked for a small red-haired woman as I strolled, until I realised she would probably be back at her typewriter already.

So I went home, where Palmer informed me that Mother was out paying calls, asked for a cup of tea to be brought to my room, and went upstairs. And with hands that shook just a little, I drew the letter from its envelope.

Chapter 3
Katherine

It was still raining when I left the restaurant. I didn't often have lunch at all, but it had been cold in the office and I had a half-baked plan to go to a lecture in the evening if Aunt Alice didn't fuss, which would mean no time for dinner. I had been halfway through that loathsome stew when I remembered I needed money to place an advertisement in the *Times*. I had already wasted the cost of purchasing a copy to establish how to do it. Not just cash but time. I checked my watch. I couldn't be late back to work. I would have to send my advertisement by post rather than at the newspaper offices.

But just as I was realising I should have missed lunch and used the money to buy a postal order and a stamp, this socialite swanned in and sat down as if it was the Ritz.

What on earth was someone like that doing in this restaurant? I thought. *I don't want to be here, why on earth would she?*

But there she was, Lady Fancy with her beautiful coat and skirt, her proper bosom supported by (no doubt) a fashionable corset, expensive shoes peeping from under a heavily trimmed skirt, her pretty eyes, her lovely hat. She made me feel like a skinny child. She was so tall, womanly and confident, complaining about her clothes while I sat like a bedraggled illustration from an article on thrift in a Woman's Weekly.

When she started kicking me, I stormed out of the restaurant and into the street, daring the rain to wet me any further. A few minutes later I marched into the post office.

I asked for paper and an envelope and, ignoring the tutting behind me, began my letter. 'I would like to place an advertisement…'

I paused, trying to remember those beautifully-planned words which had made so much sense in my head. But I had to pay for them and every word counted. The hands of the clock on the wall reached two with a clunk. My lunch break was over.

'The words I wish you to place are: "Black Tulips available from Miss K Demeray address as before",' I wrote.

The clerk was expressionless as I handed over most of my remaining coins and scurried away.

Back in the Department, I hung my dripping coat to the sound of clacking typewriters, and met the glare of Miss Charles, the supervisor.

I paused.

'Miss Demeray,' she said, 'Whatever is it? You are already late.'

I opened my bag and pulled out my purse. Now that my temper had subsided, I had time to think. As I feared, there

14

was insufficient money for any kind of fare home.

'Are you unwell?'

'No, Miss Charles.' I felt foolish. The whole thing had burned in my head all the dull morning because I had had no time to think, and now it seemed ridiculous. Why would anyone choose Father to write to in extremis?

Father's travels tended to be prompted by something he'd read: the search for Inca gold, dragons in China, genies in Arabia; but at other times, he chased after mysteries someone had put before him: lost fortunes, illustrious (and usually mythical) ancestors. The search was to him, perhaps more interesting than the unlikely possibility of success. His books and his lectures told of wild adventures, strange encounters, mysterious tales and, almost always, the answer tantalisingly out of reach, ready to be sought again. However he had, to my knowledge, never sought the same thing twice.

I tried to recall why he had gone to Anatolia. Had he ever mentioned tulips? It seemed an odd place to go, if so. But he had left no plan, no itinerary, and we had not heard from him for three years. In his absence, what could I possibly do? Why had I not gone straight to the police and saved myself a walk home in the rain? Had the letter really been that urgent? Yet it had seemed so desperate.

I reached into the bag to reread it. I couldn't find it. I turned everything out: my purse, my book, my pencil and notebook, but the letter was gone.

'Miss Demeray,' said Miss Charles, 'do sit down. You look fit to faint.'

I restrained myself from glaring at her. I turned to rummage in the pockets of Father's awful mackintosh. Nothing.

15

'I left something in the restaurant,' I said.

The supervisor narrowed her lips.

'Please, Miss Charles,' I said, 'may I have ten minutes to go out again? I will work an extra half an hour.'

'No. You will have to wait till the end of the day. We have a job to do and I will not have the men saying that women are flighty and unreliable.'

There was nothing I could do but sit down and type.

***

At five on the dot I rushed out of the Department and ran to the restaurant. The lunch-time waiters had long gone and no one recalled a letter left lying about. I retraced my steps to the post office, peering into the puddles and horse droppings, but I found nothing and the post office was shut.

By the time I got home, damp and footsore, I had run through a thousand scenarios in which my incompetence had led to something terrible happening to the letter-writer. The advertisement would not be placed until tomorrow at the earliest. If I had gone to the police…

The door was wrenched open before I'd finished trudging up the steps.

'Oh my dear!' exclaimed Aunt Alice, hauling me inside to drip on the mat. 'Wherever have you been?'

Ada appeared and helped me out of the coat. 'And there was me so proud of the shine I got on the floor this morning,' she muttered.

Aunt Alice unpinned my sodden hat and I let my hair down. It fell in damp frizziness.

'You'll catch your death,' said Aunt Alice.

'I'm going to change,' I said.

'Not yet,' said Aunt Alice, 'you have a visitor.'

For one ridiculous moment my heart bounced. Henry?

That was what she used to say when he came to call. 'You have a visitor.' But her face was more anxious than playful. And then I recalled that Henry was with Father, lost somewhere on their travels in the wide world. I wondered if *The Times* had somehow included my advertisement in the evening edition and it had borne fruit already but no, that was absurd. I looked at myself, damp and wild-haired, in the hall mirror. I tried to pin my hair back up, but it was beyond control.

'Who is it?' I whispered.

'It's a Miss Swift,' said Aunt Alice. She dropped her voice. 'Don't worry about your hair, she seems very nice. I've lit the fire and we are using the best china, but if you want a cup, you'll have to have the one with the chip.'

She opened the drawing-room door. To my astonishment, at the fireside in a different set of finery was Lady Fancy. In the lamplight and with my eyes no longer glazed with irritation, I realised she was younger than I'd thought. The bottom of her lovely skirt was damp, as if she'd been caught in the rain too. The hem had dried but the stain remained. Her thin shoes appeared uncomfortably wet. There was a nervousness about her as she sat wedged into the best chair. While it was rigid with horsehair and unpleasant to sit on, it was also built for a smaller person than Miss Swift. She looked as if she wanted to fold herself up small. I remembered our encounter and my appalling rudeness.

'I'm sorry I...' we both said.

'Miss Swift, this is my niece Miss Demeray.' Aunt Alice introduced us then turned to me. 'My dear, apparently you left something in a restaurant at lunch time and Miss Swift has kindly brought it here. We have been chatting about clothes. Miss Swift needs a good affordable dressmaker to do alterations and I wondered whom we could suggest.'

My aunt's eyes made a plea. It had been three years since we could afford a dressmaker but neither of us would admit it to a stranger.

'Oh,' I said, 'I shall check my address book later and send a message after I've thought which one is best to recommend.'

Silence fell. The clock ticked.

'I'd better find out how dinner is coming along,' said Aunt Alice. 'Miss Swift, would you care to stay?'

I imagined Miss Swift dining on a shepherd's pie made from yesterday's leftovers and bit my lip. But it was not funny. There would not be much to stretch to another person.

'Thank you, Miss Perry, but no,' said Miss Swift, 'I cannot stay. I expect Mother is . . . anxious for my return. Is it possible to hail a cab in this street, do you know?'

'I'll send Ada directly,' said Aunt Alice and left the room.

Miss Swift struggled out of the chair and stood up. I couldn't believe I had thought her confident. Now that I was calmer I could recognise the desperate shyness which meant she slumped her shoulders as if trying to shrink. All the same, if she'd stood straight and proud, she could have worn Father's coat with aplomb. She handed me the letter.

'I couldn't help but read its contents,' she said, 'I'm sorry. I brought it as fast as I could. I had to slip out and find a cab. I'm not very familiar with that sort of thing. I did look for you in the street near the restaurant first, but I couldn't see you and so I came here. But the cab took me to the wrong end of the street and I had to walk. I wouldn't have stayed but your aunt insisted I dried out. It wasn't until I arrived that I remembered who R Demeray must be and that he is missing presumed . . . missing.' She tailed off and started again, 'I have read his books. They were very thrilling.'

It seemed a strange response from someone whose life must be quite luxurious. Here was a young woman who must want for nothing, excited at the idea of travelling in foreign climes, sleeping in tents and dusty shacks, sitting on the ground to share bread with strangers. But perhaps she was bored.

'Yes,' I said, 'my father writes wonderful books.'

The clock ticked. We heard the front door open and Ada let out a piercing whistle to hail a cab. I imagined Aunt Alice wincing as she wrung her hands and hoped the neighbours hadn't heard such uncouth behaviour.

'What are you going to do?' said Miss Swift. 'Will you advertise in the *Times*?'

'I already have,' I said.

'Then what?' She was anxious, leaning forward, clasping her pretty handbag. 'That poor woman, I am so afraid for her.'

'I don't know,' I confessed. 'I am afraid too. It's partly why I was so rude earlier. I apologise.'

'I didn't mean to kick you. I'm sorry. I am so clumsy,' she said, hunching inside her lovely clothes and staring at the floor. She raised her eyes.

Please don't bend down to bring your face to my level, I thought. She didn't.

'No, really,' I said, 'it was unforgivable of me but I had a lot on my mind.'

'Cab's here Miss,' said Ada, barging into the room, 'not a moment too soon. Don't mind me, I've got a dinner to rescue from being completely ruined.' She barged back out.

I followed Miss Swift to the door. The rain had reduced to a light drizzle, still enough to make my hair a tangled mess. In the road, the horse champed and stamped and the cabbie clicked his tongue at it.

Miss Swift started down the steps and turned. We were nearly eye to eye.

'It must have been so exciting travelling with your father,' she said. 'You must have had such a wonderful life.'

'He wouldn't take me,' I said. 'I'm just a girl. But now this has happened and there's only me here to sort it out.'

She pressed a card into my hand. 'Include me,' she said, 'please include me. We needn't "just be girls". You needn't be on your own. Please. I want to help.'

CHAPTER 4
Connie

I thought I'd got away with it.

The cab drew up ten yards from the door, just as I had instructed. I got out, walked towards the house, and glanced at my watch. Twenty minutes until dinner. Everyone would be dressing except Father, who would be ensconced in his study. So long as no one happened to be crossing the hall as I came in, all should be well.

I tapped the lion's head knocker very, very carefully against the door. I heard a commotion of footsteps, and then I knew.

I was in trouble.

The door opened to reveal the stricken face of Palmer and, advancing like a queen on a chessboard, the furious figure of my mother.

'Where have you been?' she shouted. 'What have you been doing? And no lies, my girl.'

'I've been — I've been —'

'Where have you been?' She took hold of my arms as if

21

she were about to shake me.

Helena came running down the stairs. 'Oh Connie, we were so worried! No one knew where you'd gone — why didn't you tell anybody?'

'Well?' demanded my mother.

'I — um…'

'Out with it!' She seized my arm.

'I was seeing about a dressmaker,' I gabbled.

Her grip tightened. 'A dressmaker,' she said, and her voice dripped with scorn. 'You seriously expect me to believe that you sneaked out of the house alone to visit a dressmaker. At this hour!'

'She's very busy!' I cried. 'It was the only time she could fit me in.' I could feel my cheeks burning, and my palms were clammy.

Mother's eyes narrowed. 'Take off your things, and I shall see you in the morning room.' She turned to Palmer, hovering in the background. 'Palmer, tell Cook to serve dinner at the usual time. This shouldn't take long.' She swept down the corridor, and the morning-room door closed with a firm snap.

I fumbled at the fastenings of my cloak, and Palmer rushed forward to catch it. 'Can you ring for Mary, and ask her to brush it,' I muttered, pulling my hatpins out and laying the hat on the hall table. My voice sounded dull, as if the shine had gone from my day. And I feared it had.

'Stay calm, Connie,' Helena whispered. 'And try not to fidget. You know how Mother hates it.'

I clenched my fists as I walked the path of doom to the morning room. Just so long as I didn't cry. I raised my hand to tap on the door —

'Enter!' commanded my mother.

She was seated at the table, facing me, and indicated the chair opposite. 'Sit,' she said, lacing her knuckles together in front of her on the table.

I slid into a chair, which creaked.

'Explain yourself.'

I took a deep breath. 'I tried to find a dress all morning, but everyone said I was the wrong shape for ready-made, and I would need something bespoke, and I came across a lady who mentioned a possible dressmaker, and so I went to see her.'

'You went to see her.' One eyebrow went up. 'On your own, in a cab, without telling anyone.'

'Er, well, I wanted to make sure she could help before I bothered you with the matter, Mother. I know you're busy —'

'Enough.' Mother said. 'Where does this dressmaker live?'

'Mulberry Avenue, in Fulham.'

'Mmm.' My mother considered. 'And what arrangement did you arrive at?'

'We didn't settle on anything —'

'So what did you talk about, in all the time you were gone?' Mother's eyes bored into me.

'We were discussing my requirements, and she thinks she can adapt one of my old dresses to look fashionable.'

'So, of course, you have a repeat appointment? Or is she coming to the house?'

'I said I would visit her at a client's house, tomorrow.'

'That sounds satisfactory,' said my mother, unclasping her hands and laying them flat on the table. 'Provided the client is respectable.' I let my pent-up breath out in tiny instalments. 'Ring for a servant, would you.'

23

'Of course, Mother.' I tugged the bell-pull and Agnes, the smirking parlourmaid from this morning, appeared, starched beyond reproach.

'Agnes, I wish to send a telegram. Fetch pen and paper, please.' The maid withdrew.

'A — a telegram?' I stammered.

'Yes, a telegram,' Mother said briskly. 'It's always as well to confirm these things, isn't it?' And she smiled like a cat with a mouse between its paws.

'There,' she said, as Agnes returned, laying her letter-case on the table. She selected a piece of notepaper and uncapped her fountain pen, considering the blank page. 'To...?'

'The client is Miss Demeray,' I said, my heart sinking.

'Demeray,' Mother repeated, writing it down. She paused. 'Any relation to Roderick Demeray, the author?'

I swallowed. 'I believe so.'

Mother regarded me coolly, then returned to her note. 'Please confirm time of appointment tomorrow by return. Swift.' She looked up. 'The address, please.'

She was really going to do it. I repeated the address. 'Splendid,' she said, completing the postal district with a flourish. 'Ring again, please. I'm sure one of the footmen can run this down to the telegraph office.'

When William arrived she merely said, 'Send this at once, and make sure they understand I expect a reply. When it comes, bring it to me.' As soon as he left the room her eyes locked on me. 'Go and get ready for dinner. You aren't fit to be seen.'

'Yes, Mother,' I muttered, and nearly upset the chair in my haste to be out of her sight.

My heart thumped as I submitted to Mary's

ministrations. 'Look at your hair, Miss Connie, I shall have to take it down and redo it. Where have you been to get yourself into such a mess?'

'Mind your own business,' I retorted, and she lapsed into a sulky silence, relieving her injured feelings by dragging the brush through my hair.

At least the pain was a distraction from what would happen later. What if another member of the household received the telegram, and sent an answer that they had no idea what Mother meant? I saw William entering the dining room, the pause in conversation as all eyes turned towards the interruption, and Mother's face darkening as she received the message, followed by — I knew not what.

I barely tasted the salmon mousse at dinner, though when I looked down my plate was clear. 'Just one cutlet, Miss Connie?' Palmer asked, in surprise, his tongs hovering above the silver platter.

'Perhaps two,' I said. I did not want either, but I must strive to appear normal, untroubled. I dared not look at Mother.

It happened as the table was being cleared. The light tap, followed by William, bearing a small slip of paper. My mother read it, and glanced at me. 'Very well. Although not particularly convenient for dinner.' She folded the slip and gave it to the footman. 'Pass this to Miss Connie, please.' Her eyes met mine, and I could tell that, despite her use of my family pet name, I was still very much a Constance in her opinion.

The pencilled slip said *7.00 p.m., Miss K Demeray*. I put it by my side plate. I presumed K was Roderick Demeray's daughter. I wondered what the K stood for. Whatever it was, she'd saved my neck.

The next day passed with terrible slowness. The only relief was that I managed to retrieve Father's *Times* from his study, and found the advertisement. What did 'Black Tulips' mean? I hoped we would have an answer soon. The burden of dress-buying lifted, I spent the day going through my wardrobe, selecting two dresses which would not be too implausible as renovation projects. 'Such a shame,' tutted Mary, as she packed them up. 'A young lady like you shouldn't have to make do.' I wondered how the news had reached her; by the servant telegraph, I presumed.

At last it was time to leave for my appointment. Mary helped with my hat and cloak, while William put my parcels into the carriage and Palmer helped me in. 'I'll make sure Cook keeps some dinner warm for you, miss,' he whispered hoarsely. Mother, having issued curt instructions earlier that day about exactly how much she was prepared to allow me to spend, was nowhere to be seen. Hodgkins lifted the box down for me and rang the bell. 'I'll call back at a quarter past eight. Your mother thought that would be plenty of time.'

'Could you make it half past?' I asked, but the last part of my question was drowned out by the crack of his whip.

Ada, the maid, answered the door. I had hoped it would be Miss Demeray, but perhaps she was not home from work yet. It didn't matter, I could wait.

'We are busy tonight,' she remarked.

'Are we?'

The maid opened the door wider, and I set a foot on the threshold. 'You're our second caller this evening.'

My breath caught in my throat. 'And — and the first?' I asked.

Ada motioned me in and closed the door. 'She came all in a flurry,' she whispered, eyes gleaming, 'she wouldn't give me her name. But she asked me to tell Miss Katherine that she'd come about the tulips.'

Chapter 5
Katherine

The visitor was not at all what I expected.

When the door-bell rang at ten to seven, I assumed it was Miss Swift. She struck me as someone who would be so anxious not to cause offence by being late that she'd turn up early and be inconvenient instead. But it was not Miss Swift.

The woman whom Ada ushered into Father's study was bony. She was taller than I by at least five inches and yet when we shook hands she made me feel like an inelegant lump. Her gloved hand felt as fragile as a sparrow's foot; I would have been afraid of crushing it had her grip not been painfully tight. Her face was also very thin, her nose pointed, and her hair under a neat hat adorned with a bird's wing was dark and sleek.

'I've come about the tulips,' she said. Her small eyes darted round the room taking in the books and pictures as if valuing them for the bailiff, then settled on my face to do the same with me.

It was all I could do not to back away.

'It's very cold in here,' I said. It was true. The room was unheated since the only person who ever used the study was me. However it was not just the lack of heat which made me shiver. Somehow this person made me uneasy. We were both small women and yet her presence seemed to fill the study. 'Shall we retire to the drawing room?'

She gave a tiny shrug and followed me into the hallway. Aunt Alice was hindering Ada with the washing up in the kitchen, and my sister Margaret was in the dining room with her arithmetic homework, trying to finish it before Aunt Alice came to hinder her as well. Miss Robson had retired to her room as she always did after dinner. The drawing room, for an hour perhaps, would be mine.

My visitor sat down in the same chair that Miss Swift had struggled in and looked around the drawing room in the same appraising manner, clearly finding our belongings below contempt. It made me long to gather up all our old beloved things and hug them.

'About the tulips,' she said. 'You are Miss Demeray?'

'Yes,' I said. 'I wasn't expecting a reply so quickly, Miss er...'

'Armitage. I am interested in tulips. Especially black ones.'

'May I ask why particularly, Miss Armitage?'

'They're symbolic. What is your interior, Miss Demeray?'

Before I could answer, the door-bell rang again.

I heard Ada clumping up the hall and stepped out of the room, willing the ornaments not to run away.

Ada was muttering to herself. 'Of course, I got nothing better to do than hike up and down this blooming hallway. Flipping butler, that's what we need. Strange women gadding about in the evening. What's the world coming to?' She unlatched the door.

On the threshold stood Miss Swift, up to her ears in bundles. She opened her mouth but, I pressed my finger to my lips and hoped she'd understand she should keep quiet. It was bad enough Miss Armitage knew who I was; I didn't want to compromise Miss Swift too.

'Ah, here you are Miss . . . Fleet, do give your things to my maid.' Despite Ada's raised eyebrows, I shifted Miss Swift's bundles into her arms until they obscured her angry face. I whispered 'sorry' and turned her to point in the direction of the kitchen.

'Miss Fleet,' I said, 'do come into the drawing room and meet my visitor, Miss Armitage.'

Miss Swift's lips parted, then closed, and her eyes lit up. I shook my head and put my fingers to my lips again. She raised her eyebrows, but followed me into the room. I wondered how much she had gathered and hoped her eagerness would not over-ride her shyness, but I had forgotten her upbringing. By the time she greeted the other woman, Miss Swift's face was a perfect mask of well-bred indifference.

'This is my friend Miss Fleet. Miss Fleet, this is Miss Armitage.'

'How do you do.'

'How do you do.'

Miss Armitage shook hands, ran her eyes down Miss Swift's expensive attire and well-fed form and turned to me.

'About the tulips,' she said.

'Of course,' I said, 'do wait here.' I caught Miss Swift's eye, and she gave me the tiniest smile.

I left the room and took Miss Armitage back into the study. The fire had started to warm it and as I opened the door, soft smells of leather, tobacco and good books wafted. I felt a lump in my throat and half expected to find Father there, but of course he was not. I withdrew a package from a cupboard and returned to the drawing room.

'Here you are,' I said, handing the wrapped bundle to Miss Armitage.

She hesitated. For the first time doubt crossed her face but she took it and removed the string and brown paper. Inside was an old painting of a pot of tulips. The varnish was cracked and dirty, the flowers various shades of brown. It would take an expert to reveal the vibrancy hidden in two centuries of soot and grime. But it was clear that the bowl of tulips included three black ones contrasting with others which ought to be yellow or white.

'Oh,' she said.

'That was what you wanted, wasn't it?'

'Of course.' She stood up, then rummaged in her purse, handing over two shillings. 'Was that all you were offering?'

'Were you expecting anything else?'

'No. No, of course not. Good evening, ladies.' Miss Armitage re-wrapped the picture and walked briskly past Ada and out of the house. She pattered down the steps and hailed a cab.

'Why...' said Miss Swift.

'Quick,' I said, 'have you any money? We must follow

her.'

I grabbed my own coat and hat and ran down the steps. The next cab ignored me but stopped for Miss Swift. We clambered aboard and I cried 'Follow that cab!' The cabbie looked askance but complied, and we rattled off in pursuit.

'I am utterly confused,' said Miss Swift.

'I'm sorry, I couldn't explain without her overhearing,' I said.

'Didn't she come in answer to your advertisement?'

'It seems so.'

Miss Swift was silent for a moment. The horse picked up pace and we were flung sideways as the cab changed direction.

'I have to say,' said Miss Swift, 'she wasn't what I was expecting.'

'No,' I said, 'that's what I thought. The woman who wrote the letter seemed terrified. I doubt if the woman who visited this evening has ever been frightened in her whole life.'

'So you don't think they're the same person?'

'No, but I think Miss Armitage, if that's her name, knows the letter-writer. I just don't know how.'

'Why do you think Armitage is not her name?'

'Just a feeling.'

'What does it say on her visiting card?'

'She didn't give us one.'

Miss Swift gasped as if this was as unthinkable as going out with bare legs.

'But you gave her the black tulips,' she said.

'No I didn't. As soon as I saw her, I knew something about her was wrong; the person who wrote the letter was quite different. I found that painting in a flea market one lunchtime ages ago. I had some sort of half-baked plan to clean it and sell it on. It cost me sixpence so I've made a profit. Mind you,' I remembered the way she'd looked at our house, 'I have a feeling that she'll make a bigger one when she sells that picture on. I'm sure it wasn't what she expected but she wouldn't admit it. So the real black tulips must be something else.'

I paused for breath. 'I've no idea who Miss Armitage is, but she made me uneasy. I thought if I gave her something she'd think she'd got it wrong, and maybe that would keep the letter-writer safe till we can find her. I didn't want to drag you in too far without explaining. It's why I called you Fleet instead of Swift. It was the first thing that came to mind.' It wasn't. The first thing that had come to mind was Lady Fancy, but even *I* can control my mouth occasionally.

The cab lurched, and the sound of the road changed as we bounced across cobbles and potholes. The horse slowed and then stopped. I could hear the other cab disappearing into the distance.

'Miss,' called the cabbie.

We peered out of our respective windows. I had rarely been far from home even when Father wasn't missing, but I'd never been to an area like this before. Dirty water and worse lay in the gutters and potholes. Houses with broken and boarded windows closed in around us. Barely a flicker of candlelight came from most of them. Bedraggled women stood under the street lamps and huddles of men lurked in shadows beyond them. They were turning towards us. I saw the gleam of cigarettes and a flash of something metallic.

'Miss, I don't know where you think you're going,' said

the cabbie, 'but my conscience won't let me take you two ladies any further.'

'He's right,' said Miss Swift, 'we've lost her anyway, and for all we know she's taking us on a wild goose chase.' She raised her voice. 'Thank you, driver. Please could you take us back?'

The cab turned and we started for home. I slumped. Had I got it all wrong?

Miss Swift sighed, 'You did the right thing, but,' she paused, 'if you don't mind my saying so, I think we should sit down with the letter and see what we can work out from it. For example, where was it postmarked?'

I felt a fool. I hadn't even thought of looking. I had been so busy rushing ahead.

It was time to start again.

CHAPTER 6
Connie

'Oh my goodness, it's almost eight o'clock!'

Miss Demeray put a hand on my arm. 'We're nearly home. We can make a pot of tea and talk it ov —'

The cab lurched and her hand was jerked away. 'No, we can't!' I rapped on the roof of the cab. 'Fast as you can, please! I'll pay you double!' The whip cracked, and the cab's rolling grew faster and faster, as if I were trapped in a terrible dream.

When I looked back, Miss Demeray was regarding me rather oddly. 'The carriage is coming for me at a quarter past eight,' I explained, feeling foolish. 'I can't be late.'

Her eyes widened. 'Why not?'

'If Hodgkins sees that I haven't been at your house having a dress fitting, then Mother will get to know. Even if he doesn't tell her directly, she'll find out somehow.'

'And then?'

'No more evening visits. Probably no dinner parties or entertainments, since I don't have anything to wear. And no more mystery.'

The cab slowed, and she raised the window-blind. 'Here we — oh.'

The carriage was already waiting.

'Shut the blind.' I leaned across and did it myself. 'Does your house have a back door?'

'Yes, of course, it leads into the back garden and then into the alley.'

'Here's what we do. You get out, I'll pay, and the cab can take me round. You go through the house, and look out for me from the alley. Tell Ada to stall Hodgkins.'

Miss Demeray's eyes flicked over me. 'You're really scared, aren't you?' Her voice was kind.

'I don't want to be shut up at home for the rest of my life, so yes. Yes, I am.'

'I'll do my best —'

'Wait — pull your hat down, so he can't see your face.'

She raised her eyebrows, but did as I asked. Then she opened the door, and was gone.

I paid the cabman, adding an extra half-crown for good measure. 'Can you take me round to the back entrance, please? Not too fast, just as if you were heading to the main road.'

He clicked to the horse, and we set off at what seemed like a snail's pace compared to our mad gallop earlier. We turned left about a hundred and fifty yards down the road, and the cab stopped.

'This is as far as I can go, ma'am,' he called. 'The alley is on your left. If I carry on down here for a bit, I can get to the high street without passing the house again.'

'Thank you so much.' My knees gave way as I stepped down, and I clutched at the door handle, leaning on the cab for support.

'Are you sure you're all right, miss?' The cabman was leaning down from his box.

'Yes, yes of course,' I said, standing upright. 'I'm quite all right. Just — a bit stiff.'

'My cab number is 324,' he muttered, 'and my name's Sam Webster. You can find me at the cabmen's shelter in Leicester Square.' He paused, and the cab lamp showed that under his cap and greatcoat he was much younger than I had thought. I had always assumed that cab drivers were grizzled veterans, but he looked no more than thirty. 'I don't know why I'm telling you this, miss, but I have a feeling it may be useful. Now get yourself back to where you should be.'

'Where were we tonight, when you stopped?' I asked.

'That was St Giles,' he said. 'Not a safe place for a young lady like you to venture.'

'No,' I said. 'Thank you.' He touched his cap, and I set off down the alley, my boots sliding on the wet paving. It was dark, and the alley smelt of cats, but at last I saw a small white thing moving from side to side through a gate, which resolved itself into Miss Demeray's waving hand.

'Was everything all right? I was worried,' she said.

'I was talking to the cabman,' I said, in the manner of one who had been conducting an investigation, and had not been scared at all. 'He said he stopped the cab at St Giles. And he told me where I could find him.'

Miss Demeray's brow furrowed for an instant, then cleared. 'He probably wants more business from you. You're a generous tipper. Now come on.' She led me down the path to the house. The back door stood open showing a small kitchen. 'We have fifteen minutes. Your driver rang

37

the bell at eight o'clock precisely, and Ada, bless her, told him you were having your hem pinned and wouldn't be available until twenty past eight at the earliest. She said he looked rather alarmed.'

'I imagine he did,' I said, sighing with relief as Miss Demeray closed the door behind us.

Ada, our saviour, was lifting a kettle from the hob, and a large brown teapot stood ready. 'You'll have to have it in the family cups,' she said. 'I haven't had time to get the best set out, not with all this back and to.' But the corners of her mouth were turned up.

'I'd drink it out of a shoe, and be grateful,' I said. 'It's been quite an evening.'

Her mouth tightened. 'That won't be necessary,' she said, stirring the pot.

'We'll be in the study, Ada,' said Miss Demeray, firmly, escorting me out.

The lady I had conversed with about dresses on my last visit was hovering in the hallway. 'I hope you don't mind, Miss Swift,' she said, her blue eyes anxious, 'but your parcels had come undone and I looked inside. The blue velvet is lovely.'

'But last season,' I said flatly. 'Skirts are gored now.'

'Yes, yes they are,' she said. 'But it would be possible to add panels. I saw some material today in a lovely shade of heliotrope. I understand from Katherine that you are in a hurry, and perhaps a dressmaker might not have time. I'd be happy to do it for a friend of hers, if you'd like. Oh, and I could trim the bodice to match, and square the neckline.'

I glanced at Miss Demeray. 'Aunt Alice is a very good needlewoman,' she said quietly.

'Miss Perry, that would be so kind,' I said, 'but how

long would it take you to do all that?'

'Assuming the dress doesn't need any extra fitting,' she said, 'I could probably have it ready for tomorrow evening.'

I blinked. 'How much would that cost, with the new material, and the work?'

'Perhaps . . . two pounds for the material? Nothing of course for the work. It will be a pleasure.'

'Two pounds?' I cried. 'Is that all? But you can't do all that work for nothing...' I could see her face close and a blush rise. The last thing I wanted was to humiliate her, but it seemed so wrong to let her do the work for nothing. I thought quickly.

'Of course I won't need any of the spare material, like the old panels and flounces,' I said. 'Please do keep them. They are far too good to go to waste.'

She brightened a little.

'Yes, I could make good use of them. Thank you...' Her voice tailed off into a smile. 'I'll purchase the material first thing tomorrow.'

'And I'll give you the money now.' I opened my bag.

'Oh no, no, that won't be necessary —'

'I want to. You've helped me out of a terrible mess. And if the dress is ready, I can return tomorrow.'

Ada appeared with a tray. 'I thought you said you'd be in the study,' she said, her eyes settling on us each in turn.

'We'll use the drawing room,' said Miss Demeray. 'That will give us a little more time.' She gave her aunt a significant look.

'I'll fetch my workbox,' said Miss Perry, and vanished upstairs.

This time I chose the settee. Miss Demeray and I looked

at each other as Ada set down the tray and withdrew.

'Thank you, Miss Demeray,' I said. 'I would have been in so much trouble if you hadn't played along with my telegram.'

'That's all right,' she said, to the teapot. 'I'll pour out. Aunt Alice will do a wonderful job. I'd forgotten how expensive ballgown material was.'

'It isn't so much,' I said. 'It's less than I'd have paid for a ready-to-wear dinner dress.'

Her green gaze held me for a second. Something told me two pounds was a good deal more than Katherine earned in a week. She sighed. 'What should we do next?'

'Lots of things,' I said, counting on my fingers. 'Try and find out what "black tulips" mean, perhaps; they definitely meant something to Miss Armitage. That painting of yours looked awfully familiar. I'm wondering why the cabman told me where to find him, because I don't think he knew himself. Oh, and St Giles could be important. We could check it against the postmark on your letter.' A bright thought dawned, and I snapped my fingers. 'Maybe the letter-writer will call tomorrow, or even tonight, and explain some of the mystery! That would be very helpful.'

Miss Demeray looked doubtful. 'Perhaps. She might have missed the advertisement, since she didn't call today.'

'Or she might have had a previous engagement,' I said, sipping my tea.

'Perhaps I should advertise again,' she mused.

'Do you need money for that?' I said, reaching for my bag.

She shot me a look. 'I'll leave it a couple of days.'

'I don't mind, honestly —'

'It isn't that,' she said, and I believed her. 'It's just —
I'm not sure what we're getting into.'

The silence was broken by the jangle of the door-bell.

'That'll be Hodgkins,' I sighed. 'I'd better go before the
carriage turns into a pumpkin.' Miss Demeray smiled, and
a green light danced in her eyes.

We heard Ada bustling down the hallway, grumbling,
and the bolt on the door sliding back. 'Ah, good evening,'
she said. 'I'll see how she's getting on.'

'When shall I come tomorrow?' I whispered.

'Six o'clock,' she said, under her breath, 'to give Aunt
Alice time to finish your dress.'

'I'll try.' I rose. 'Thank you so much,' I said, in
carrying tones. 'It will look beautiful when it's finished.'

I sailed out of the room and confronted Hodgkins, who
was twisting his cap in the hallway. 'Time to go, Miss
Connie,' he said.

'Yes,' I replied. 'Time to go.'

I was glad that Hodgkins couldn't see inside as we
drove home, for I am sure I grinned all the way. I rebuked
myself, for our letter-writer could be in danger, and we had
quite possibly had a brush with danger ourselves that night.
What if the cabman had taken us into the slum? There was
nothing to smile about. And yet the fact remained that this
evening had been the most fun I had ever had.

CHAPTER 7
Katherine

Pacing the floor of the hall, checking my watch, I wondered how the rich got to be so rich when they couldn't get up. Perhaps this was unfair of me, given the number of mornings I'd longed to be wealthy enough to loll in bed rather than go to work.

I had just slipped into Father's study to check the bookshelves yet again for any reference to black or indeed any other colour of tulips, when the door-bell rang. Before I could get there Ada, as usual, appeared out of nowhere and opened it.

My cousin Albert stood on the threshold and pretended he was about to trip over the boot scraper. Ada had braced herself, ready.

'Should I paint that scraper red, Master Bertie?' said Ada as if he were eight years old. 'Do you think I'd look better if I was flat?'

'Frightfully sorry, Ada,' said Albert, lifting his hat and

stepping into the hall. They had been going through the same routine ever since he really had tripped over it. It was their private joke. He bent his head to kiss my cheek. Albert was another person who could have worn Father's coat without looking absurd. It would never have done to tell him so, but I was always surprised he hadn't been snapped up. Quite apart from his height and elegance, his blue eyes were open and frank, his smile honest, his dark hair irreproachably brushed back.

'How do, K,' he said. 'What's the emergency?'

'I need a man.'

'Oh, I say.' Albert looked terrified. 'I'm sure Henry will come back eventually.'

'Not for matrimony Albert. For propriety. And also possibly for any ready cash you might have.'

'Don't mind me,' said Ada, 'I'm just wallpaper, I am.' She stepped smartly towards the kitchen.

'I'm waiting for a friend,' I told Albert. 'She and I need an escort. Perhaps she more than I. Her mother would only agree to our expedition if we had a respectable (by which she meant notable) man to accompany us. You're all I've got in that category. Fortunately she was impressed with your family's antecedents and my friend will be here any moment.'

'Does "mother" know I'm an impoverished youngest son?'

'I didn't think it worth mentioning. As long as you're suitable for my friend that's all that matters.'

'I'm not sure which is worse,' said Albert pulling a face, 'a snob or a blue-stocking.'

'Connie's neither, don't worry.' I heard a familiar rattle of wheels. 'That'll be her. It's ten to nine and I told her nine o'clock. I told *you* eight thirty.'

'Yes but eight thirty is practically the middle of the night K,' he said as I opened the door.

Connie's carriage had pulled up on the other side of Albert's. It was impossible to think of her as Miss Swift after Tuesday. Once we'd shared a pot of tea in the third-best chipped teacups, she was pretty much family.

Hodgkins acknowledged Albert's driver with a touch to his cap and the two coachmen sized up the coats of arms on each other's doors before Hodgkins got down, presumably to help Connie alight.

'Come along, Albert,' I said, starting down the steps. 'We'll get into your coach and sit there until Connie's leaves.'

'What will you do then?'

'Unless you'd like to escort us there, we'll get out of your carriage and go into town.'

'On your own?'

'Well, yes. But we don't want Connie's mother knowing that.' I took a deep breath, 'Could you lend me ten shillings? I'm not sure how much the tube is.'

'The tube?'

'The underground train.'

'I know what the tube is. But K, you can't do that on your own. You're a lady. You're too…' His face worked as he struggled for a word, 'delicate?' We were on the pavement and Connie was coming towards us. Albert turned his attention from me and blinked. She was as pretty as ever, the rich red of her outfit brightening her face — or possibly she was blushing. Her neat hat sat on her full, light brown hair, tipped forward over her blue eyes.

'Oh for pity's sake Albert,' I said. 'May I introduce you

to my friend Miss Constance Swift. Connie, may I introduce my cousin, Mr Albert Lamont.'

I have to admit, for a moment I felt something of a fool standing next to them. Connie's carriage was pulling away, while Albert's waited for us. Connie was tall and fashionable, and although she'd ducked her head slightly as usual, she had to straighten up to greet Albert properly since he, dressed in the smartest clothes Savile Row could offer, was at least three inches taller than she was. Meanwhile, I, in my tired old office clothes, barely came up to Albert's shoulder. From a distance I must have looked like their child.

Before I could break into the silence that had fallen after the hand-shaking and hat-raising, the postman brought the second post.

'Here's one for you Miss.' He handed me a letter, then went up the steps to the house.

'Is it…?' said Connie.

I turned it over. 'Yes.'

My heart thudded.

'Same postmark?'

I peered but it was too smudged to tell.

'Will you please tell me what's going on?' said Albert.

'If you'd arrived on time this morning, I'd have told you,' I said. 'But now there's no time. I can't afford to waste a day's leave. If Hodgkins is safely out of sight, we can start into town. Connie, my apologies but do you mind if I have a private word with my cousin?'

I drew Albert aside. 'Just ten shillings, Albert, I promise I'll return whatever I don't use and pay back what I owe.'

Albert frowned. 'You know Father would help if you'd let him. You don't have to do all this penny pinching.'

'He is already paying for Margaret's school fees. I can't ask for more. We can manage on what I can earn until Father . . . until Father returns. Could you spare ten shillings? I know it's a lot. I, er, sold something for two the other day which meant I could take a day's leave, but I do need money for expenses today. I promise I'll pay you back.'

Albert was silent for a moment. I thought he was looking at the ground, then realised he was sneaking glances at Connie. The letter burned in my hand.

'K,' he said eventually, 'I'll *give* you the money if you'll let me take you both in the carriage to wherever you want to go. Or,' a thought struck him, 'I may even come on the tube with you. I'm all for new experiences — with the exception of having to be somewhere at eight thirty a.m. But you have to give me some idea of what you're doing. Are you in trouble?'

'No,' I said. But the memory of Miss Armitage's sharp face and small eyes made me shiver.

'Come along ladies,' he said a little more loudly as he opened the door of the carriage for Connie, 'where are we bound?'

I noted he made rather more effort to help Connie aboard than he did me, but perhaps he owed me for all the times I kicked him when we were children.

Settled inside, I told him: 'Kensington. Science Museum, National Museum, Natural History Museum and if there's time, the National Gallery.'

He groaned, 'All of them? That'll give us intellectual indigestion. I mean, I'm sorry Miss Swift, I suppose you're a brain like K.'

'No, not at all,' Connie peered up from under the edge

of her hat, 'Mother thinks I'm... Anyway, we're doing some research into, er... Anyway, it is very pleasant to make your acquaintance, Mr Lamont.'

'Do call me Albert.'

'Connie.'

They relapsed into silence but I nudged Connie and we moved closer to the window so that we could look at the envelope. Neither of us could make out the postmark, so it was impossible to tell where or when the letter had been dispatched. The previous one had been posted in Hendon. But the tulips nagged at me. I'd spent the previous evening, and most of the morning before Albert's arrival, consulting Father's books. The trouble was that his library covered everything from ancient Mesopotamian idol worship to Darwinism, and from Islamic texts about the four humours to the use of ether in operations. Not one single book was in any kind of order. And Connie had seen something in that grubby little painting which made her wonder if I should have handed it over to Miss Armitage so eagerly. On the other hand, at least I had two shillings to cover my loss of wages.

'Come on Katherine,' said Connie, 'we must open it.'

'What if we've put her in...?' I glanced at my cousin and fell silent.

'Put who in what?' asked Albert. We ignored him and I opened the envelope.

Within was another single sheet of paper. The writing was, if anything, more agitated.

Dear Miss Demeray,

I know you put an advertisement in The Times, even though when they let me see the paper, the personal notices had been removed. Every single one. I knew from this that you must have replied. Why else would they have removed the pages? Unless it was to taunt me of course. It has been so many years since anyone tried to trace me that I am no longer sure I exist. You do not know what they are like. The Magpie is like a gimlet. The Viper is . . . unspeakable.

And yet, how would they know it was to me that you appealed? I fear they may have read your name and address on the blotter. I should have destroyed it. But perhaps they are not so clever as they think. I remembered what happens to waste newspaper. When they were out, I found the pages rolled up in a grate, ready to start the fire. They were down among the coals but I unwrapped them and found your advertisement. If I have not managed to get all the soot from my hands, and if they guess I went outside and left a letter in someone's pocket in the hope that they would post it. I am so very afraid I shall lose even more days or perhaps years.

Miss Demeray, I do not know who you are. I assume you must be Mr Demeray's sister or daughter. I sincerely hope that all is well with him. I knew him when we were children. That seems such a long time ago. But then, I am not sure of the date anymore.

Miss Demeray, I cannot tell you where I am, because I am quite confused.

But I am begging you. ~~Roderick~~ *Mr Demeray has the answer.*

I cannot write any more. I have no paper left and I am not sure how I could post any more.

~~When they find out~~
~~If they suspect I have~~
I do not know what to do.

CHAPTER 8
Connie

'I don't know what to do, either.'

I said the words without thinking, and was greeted by silence. Two pairs of eyes regarded me. Miss Demeray — Katherine (I was still getting used to it) looked stern, while Albert seemed curious, and perhaps a little concerned.

'Is there anything we could do to help?' he asked.

I shook my head slowly, while my brain raced ahead seeking a plausible excuse. 'Oh no,' I said. 'It isn't anything to do with the letter. I was thinking of a dinner engagement I have tomorrow.'

His face cleared. 'Don't you want to go?'

Now I felt on much safer ground. 'The food will be lovely — it always is — but I have to be on my best behaviour, and I'm not very good at that.'

Albert snorted, and his shoulders shook. 'It isn't funny,' I said, feeling aggrieved.

'No, no, that isn't what I meant,' he said hastily. 'I feel exactly the same. I always have to make small talk, which I can't do. I don't like port, or brandy, so all the men smirk at me after dinner when I pass the decanter on. And if there's dancing —' he shuddered. 'I can't tell you how horrid it is.' He smiled ruefully. 'And now you've reminded me that I have to go to a dinner tomorrow night, too.'

'You poor things,' said Katherine, with a gleam in her eye.

'I won't be allowed to eat more than half of anything, you know,' I huffed. 'Half of the things I like, but also exactly half of the food I can't stand. There's always caviar at the Frobishers', and I hate the way it pops on your tongue.'

'The Frobishers?' said Albert, leaning forward. 'I'm going to the Frobishers.'

I smiled. 'At least I can be miserable in company, then.'

'No, but don't you see?' A grin spread over his face, making him look ridiculously boyish. 'We can talk to each other, and then we don't have to talk to other people. We could sit out some of the dances together. I could even kick you under the table if you're eating too much.'

'He's good at that,' said Katherine, darkly.

'I might pass on the kicking, if you don't mind,' I said. 'But the talking sounds good. Especially if it means less dancing. I always get scolded for leading, or dancing the wrong steps, or treading on my partner's toes.'

'When you two have quite finished,' said Katherine, poking me, 'we're nearly at South Kensington. Where shall we go first?'

'The Natural History Museum,' I said firmly. 'That seems like the best place to learn about tulips.'

'Tulips?' said Albert. '*Tulipa gesneriana*. But you're a

bit early, aren't you?'

I goggled at him. 'Albert,' said Katherine, rather sharply. 'Do you mean to tell me that you are an expert on tulips?'

'I wouldn't go that far,' said Albert, looking bashful. 'But tulip season starts in March. I remember doing it at school, in History. The Dutch tulip mania.'

'The Dutch tulip mania...' Katherine repeated, thoughtfully. 'Do you know, Albert, I'm beginning to revise my opinion of you.'

'Up or down?' he asked, with a sly glance at me.

'We'll see,' she said, and glanced out of the window. 'Ooh, stop the carriage, we're in Exhibition Road already.'

Albert helped me down, and I was glad of his steadying hand. I felt bewildered; on one hand as if I were floating in a bubble, but at the same time my senses were sharpened. The sky was the brightest blue it had ever been, and Albert's hand in its glove felt hot enough to burn.

And somewhere in Hendon, miles on the other side of London, our poor letter-writer was trapped and frightened, while we were in South Kensington investigating tulips.

'Are you all right?'

I blinked, and Albert was gazing into my face. 'You looked . . . rather as if you had indigestion.'

'I'm fine, thank you,' I said, with the brightest smile I could manage. 'Let's get on.'

We bustled round the Natural History Museum, passing fossils and shells and all manner of animal skeletons in our quest for tulips. Eventually, after several wrong turns, we found a display case containing tulip bulbs and a set of watercolours depicting the parts of a tulip. 'Tulips have been cultivated in almost every colour,' proclaimed the display.

'I wonder if that includes black,' mused Katherine.

A low chuckle made us turn. A few feet away, studying another part of the display, stood a man with mutton-chop whiskers. He wore a tweed knickerbocker suit and a flat cap; a cyclist, presumably. 'If you were a real tulip fancier you'd know the answer to that, miss. Growers have been trying for years to create a true black tulip. They say Krelage is the closest, but even he ain't that close.'

'A new tulip mania,' breathed Katherine.

'In a manner of speaking, my dear.' The man grinned. 'And all so the fine ladies can have black flowers in their posies.' He gave me an elaborate wink, and moved off.

I could feel myself blushing, and fanned my face discreetly. I didn't feel very fine at all. 'I don't think we'll find anything else here,' I heard myself say. 'Shall we try the South Kensington Museum?'

'Why not,' said Albert. 'It might be less dusty.'

He offered his arm for the short stroll down the road. I took it, and reflected on how pleased Mother would be if she could see me at this moment, strolling on the arm of a Lamont in fashionable South Kensington, improving my mind.

She was, for once, favourably disposed towards me. When I arrived home on Wednesday night, my newly-altered dress parcelled up in brown paper, she had been waiting for me. 'You seem pleased with yourself,' she observed.

'I think it's lovely,' I said. And I did. The new heliotrope panels lifted the heavy blue velvet, and the square neckline looked more modern and less matronly.

'Go and put it on, then,' she said. 'Let's see this two-pound dress.' Her mouth curled at the corner. 'I shall be in my boudoir.'

My hands clenched on the parcel as I carried it upstairs. I had done my best, under difficult circumstances, to do as Mother had asked, and she threw it back at me. But I hoped the dress would prove her wrong. I rang for Mary, who exclaimed as she lifted the dress out of the brown paper. 'Oh, Miss Connie, it's like the one in this week's *Illustrated London News*!'

'Not too like, I hope,' I said, as she began to unbutton me.

'Oh no, Miss,' she assured me. 'But very fashionable.'

In five minutes I was ready, with matching slippers and bag. 'I'd redo your hair,' said Mary, sadly, 'but Madame won't be kept waiting.'

'No, she won't,' I flung up my head, and strode out of the room.

'Come in,' called Mother when I was still a few steps from her room. I did as I was told, and stood while she examined me. The little curl was still at the corner of her mouth. 'Well,' she said.

I waited.

The curl broadened into a small smile. 'It actually suits you,' she said. 'And it doesn't look like a make-do. Good.'

I decided to strike while the iron was hot. 'May I go out with Miss Demeray tomorrow, to the museums?'

The smile disappeared. 'Miss Demeray?'

'Yes, Miss Demeray. She recommended a dressmaker who was visiting her house — and when we started talking we found a common interest in history.'

'And is she related to Roderick Demeray?' Mother sounded hopeful.

'Miss Demeray is his daughter, yes.' I prayed this was the right answer.

'You are friends with Roderick Demeray's daughter,' said my mother, a slightly dazed look on her face. 'Do you have someone to look after you?'

'Pardon, Mother?'

'A suitable man, to take you about?'

'Um, well, I am sure Miss Demeray could arrange —'

'See to it that she does. Get William to send a wire.' She sighed. 'You may go.'

I did as I was told, and when the reply came that her cousin Albert Lamont would accompany us, I dutifully relayed the news to Mother.

'Mr Albert Lamont. Is he one of the Lamonts, of Eaton Square?'

'I imagine so,' I said, though I had no idea who the Lamonts were.

'Good gracious,' she said, and her eyes took on a faraway look.

'So I can go?' I asked, trying not to fidget.

'Yes, yes, you may go. Make sure you behave nicely, Connie.' The bestowal of my pet name, rather than my Sunday name, was a rare concession from Mother. For once, I thought, the stars had aligned, and I had got things right.

'A penny for them,' said Albert.

'Oh, sorry,' I said, coming back to the present. 'I was miles away.'

'I could tell. You haven't said a word since we left the Natural History Museum.' But he was smiling. 'I do it all the time. Get lost in my thoughts. They're usually so much more interesting than what people are trying to say to me.'

I considered how to respond, and settled for a giggle. We were almost at the South Kensington Museum, and near the entrance I saw the square bottle-green shape of a cabmen's shelter, with a line of cabs tied up outside. I remembered Sam Webster, and thinking of the nocturnal trip to St Giles, I shivered a little.

Sadly, this museum was even less fruitful than the last. We roamed through the art galleries seeking tulips, and paintings in the same style as Katherine's bargain find, but drew a blank. 'We need to look at fine art,' I said. 'The Dutch masters, perhaps. They must have painted a tulip or two.'

'The National?' asked Katherine.

'I think so.'

'What about lunch?' asked Albert plaintively.

I consulted my watch. 'It's only half past eleven. One more try, and then lunch.' He looked just a little mutinous, like a sulky schoolboy.

It didn't take us long. Albert told his coachman to buck up, and we were there in twenty minutes. 'I shall want something substantial to eat,' grumbled Albert.

'Raw meat?' said Katherine, pointing to the lions guarding Trafalgar Square.

'Very funny.'

We went straight to the Dutch School galleries. Vermeer, Rembrandt, Frans Hals… We passed by groups of diners, moody landscapes, quiet harbours, and paused at a wall of still lifes.

Katherine gasped. 'There!' We followed her finger to a small, dim canvas high on the wall. A vase of tulips, red and yellow, on a dark background. She peered, and put her hand to her mouth. 'You can just see them.'

Katherine was right. Barely visible against the darkness, there almost as an absence, were three black shapes. Black tulips.

'Dutch School,' read Albert. 'That isn't very helpful.'

'There's something else written underneath,' I said. 'Can you see it? It's right on the edge of the frame, in small letters.'

Albert shook his head. 'I'm rather short-sighted,' he said.

'And I'm short,' growled Katherine. 'Can't you see, Connie?'

'Not quite...' I looked around. The gallery was quiet. 'You two. Go over there and cause a diversion.'

Albert raised his eyebrows.

'I don't know, argue about a painting.'

Katherine took Albert's arm and led him away. 'I don't agree,' she said, in strident tones.

I saw heads turn to follow them. *Now, Connie.* I climbed onto a bench in front of the painting. It was slightly rickety, and I put my arms out to keep my balance.

DUTCH SCHOOL
Donated by Sir Peter Langlands

'Miss!'

I turned. An attendant was hurrying over, glaring. 'Those benches are for sitting on!'

I got down. 'I'm terribly sorry,' I said demurely. 'I was just trying to see the painting a little better. It's so lovely, and I am terribly short-sighted. It's such a shame they're hung so high.'

'That's all right, madam,' said the attendant, mollified

56

now that I was back on the ground. 'We don't want anyone to come to any harm, now do we?'

'No, indeed we don't,' I said, and swept off, gathering up Katherine and Albert on the way.

'Did you see?' hissed Katherine, as we went downstairs.

'Yes,' I whispered under my breath. 'It was donated by a Sir Peter Langlands.'

'Perhaps our letter-writer knows him —'

'All right,' said Albert, stopping suddenly on the landing. 'What's going on? You two are up to something.'

Katherine glared at him. 'It isn't your business, Albert.'

His jaw clenched. 'It is if I'm squiring you about London.'

'Fine. Albert, you may go. We don't need you.' And Katherine carried on walking down the stairs.

I didn't know what to do. I didn't know whether I should follow my friend, and try and talk her round, or placate Albert, who was standing on the grand staircase, fuming.

But I couldn't catch Katherine, who was nearly at the entrance, and Albert was right there.

'We do need you,' I said. 'I need you, if I'm going to be part of this at all. Promise not to tell?'

He sighed, but looked relieved at the same time. 'All right. I promise.'

Katherine had stopped, and was waiting by the door. 'Come on,' I said to Albert. 'Let's go and find lunch.'

CHAPTER 9
Katherine

The underground would have to wait until another day. The light had gone and it was time to get Connie home.

I felt frustrated and useless. The other two had fallen into silence. Connie was looking out of the window at workers scurrying home in the dark. Soon, the London streets would be taken over by socialites off to the theatres and restaurants or to the music halls in the less salubrious parts of town. Albert was watching Connie out of the side of his eyes surreptitiously as he primed his pipe. I wished they'd both concentrate.

I turned the letter over in my hand and although I couldn't see the words, I remembered them.

I do not know what to do.

Unaccountably, my eyes filled with tears. I had not wasted time on crying for two years. Father and Henry were missing and I had had to find work to keep food on the table. Crying would not bring them back or give me a life of luxury. I was trapped, trying to find little bits of time to work out how to help the letter-writer, Connie was trapped by the demands of her mother. But neither of us were as trapped as…

She didn't even have a name, poor woman. How was it that no-one cared that she was missing? Did she have no friends? Then I realised it was over a year since any of my old friends had come to call, and there was never time to make friends in the office.

I looked sideways. Connie was next to me, all shyness and rebellion, and opposite her was Albert, all shyness and bluff. Tomorrow night they would be going to a fine dinner while Aunt Alice was scouring Mrs Beeton for something frugal to eat. They would dance, badly perhaps but they'd dance and then they would talk and be outsiders together. Meanwhile I would sit at home with a book and perhaps listen to Miss Robson accompany Aunt Alice on the piano.

No, I wouldn't.

'Miss Holland,' I said, rubbing my eyes as surreptitiously as I could.

Connie jumped. 'Who?'

'I'm calling our letter-writer Miss Holland. I don't like her being nameless, and it just seems fitting. Tulips, Dutch masters, that sort of thing.'

'You've had a letter from someone you don't know?' said Albert.

I'd forgotten he didn't know the whole story.

'Don't worry,' I said.

'Are you sure?' he replied.

'No really, don't worry,' said Connie.

He muttered something under his breath. It sounded like 'I shall if I want to.'

We arrived home seconds before Connie's carriage turned up. I bade them both goodbye on the pavement and climbed the steps to the front door. Ada opened it as I pulled out my key. 'I'm sure it's never been a good idea to cross you, Miss Kitty,' she said, 'but I own that I'm worried. What are you up to?' Only Margaret called me Kitty nowadays. As if I was too grown up for a pet name. The tears welled up again.

Ada is the only person I know who's shorter than I, but she is stronger than a cart horse. She gave me a brief, slightly painful hug and whispered in my ear. 'What would your Mr Henry do? What would your Father do? Think on that and you'll find your answer.'

***

I left the Department at five o'clock the following evening. Right now, Connie was probably being prepared for dinner at the Frobishers' like a prize pet for a show. Someone would be drying her hair and curling it and pinning it up. Someone else would be shaking out the creases in her 'new' dress. I tried not to feel envious. Meanwhile, not too far away, Albert would be doing whatever it was that men do to get ready. In Albert's case, this would most likely involve leaving it to his valet, and the last minute.

But I had my own journey to make. Telling myself to grow up, I straightened my shoulders and found the omnibus. It wasn't my usual one. Other girls from the office passed without noticing me in the queue. 'She's so stand-offish,' one said. 'Every lunchtime she beetles off with a book, never stops to chat. Who does she think she is?'

'I'm sure she's just shy,' said the other.

Their voices faded. Were they talking about me? Well, there was nothing I could do now.

I climbed aboard the omnibus and put my bag on my lap. Pulling out my small notebook, I looked through what I'd written down. For a start, my route to Hendon. I was heading out of the London I knew and needed to change omnibuses at Hampstead. Secondly, my list of thoughts and ideas.

I'd encouraged Connie to take notes too, but she had a different approach, her thoughts scattered at random angles all over the page. I would have found it irritating if it hadn't reminded me of Father. My notes were in columns: 'whereabouts', 'tulips', 'who are "they"'. So far, each column was rather sparse. A tiny voice suggested that if Connie and I simply sat down with our different approaches and actually listened to each other, we might get further.

Still, she was about to dance the light fantastic while I continued our quest. My dangling feet fidgeted. I missed dancing.

I put the notebook away and pulled out my other books. One was a small pamphlet about Hendon which I'd found on a second-hand book stall. It was about fifty years old and probably useless. London was about to swallow Hendon the way it had recently swallowed Clapham, but the leaflet suggested green rurality. I suspected I would find it very changed. However, presumably St Mary's Church was still there and would be a reference point. The second book was one of Father's. It was a study of the doctrine of signatures, setting out how a plant might have magical properties according to its appearance. Eye-bright for example, resembling tired, bloodshot eyes and used for ocular diseases. It was very old and printed in a text which was hard to read. But it had seemed like a possibility, one step more scientific than the language of flowers. I couldn't work out what body part a tulip might represent, and so far I hadn't found any reference. I couldn't really see either the leaflet or the book in the gloom.

I changed omnibuses and tried to remember what I'd been reading, but the words had slipped out of my brain. Every now and again I would observe the other passengers. By the time we neared Hendon, they had thinned out considerably. Perhaps its inhabitants were waiting until the underground train reached them before commuting.

I did notice, however, that at least three people had travelled all the way, perhaps four. A good-looking young man had got on at Shaftesbury Avenue; medium height and moustached, with dark brown hair curling under his hat. When he caught me watching him he grinned, and blushing, I longed for the old fashioned sort of bonnet you could peek from undetected. There was a middle-aged couple and an older man with a determined beard. The couple made me think of Jack Spratt and his wife. The man was very tall and slender, his coat hanging off his frame. The woman was small and round, with sparkling eyes peeping from beneath the very sort of hat I had wished for. She wasn't looking at the young man, though, but at me. I felt myself blush and studied my book.

By the time we arrived, only the five of us were left. I alighted and stood on the pavement. It was now pitch dark. The main street was busy, a number of shops still open for those who were returning from work. The church was only just visible, ghostly beyond the street lamps. I had hoped perhaps I'd be able to see some of the gravestones or that a service might be in progress and I could peruse the register, although I had no idea what name I was looking for. Without any form of light, however, it was hard to know what I could do.

'Are you lost, Miss?'

I turned and found the woman in the old-fashioned bonnet beside me. Her hand in its mitten rested on my arm.

'No. Thank you. I am quite all right.' Father had always said one should never seem lost even when one was. Henry memorised maps to be sure he wouldn't.

'Really, dear? You look a little bamboozled.' Her husband loomed alongside her and leant down to peer into my face. It was a peculiar movement, as if he was taking my whole being in as he bent. The woman's eyes were also taking me in, from the brass buttons on my coat to the buckles on my shoes, and returned to rest on the brooch fastening my scarf. Her little hand tightened on my arm.

'We wondered if you were looking for someone,' said the husband.

I couldn't help but start.

'We saw you looking at a letter from time to time,' said the woman, with a warm, bright smile. 'It's easy to get lost. We…' She and her husband shared another smile, 'we like to help lost people.'

'We do indeed,' he said. He licked his lips and bent again in that peculiar way. Her sharp little fingers pressed into my arm.

The magpie is like a gimlet and the viper is unspeakable.

'No really, I'm fine. Thank you very much.' I pulled my arm free and went into a hardware store. They did not follow me, but stood irresolute on the pavement.

'Can I help you, Miss?' said the proprietor.

'Just looking,' I replied, standing near the window and rummaging in things I did not recognise. The couple did not move. The young man from the omnibus slowed as he approached them. I couldn't be sure if they spoke or not. My view was obscured and the street lights too dim. But then the couple moved in one direction and the man in another. The woman glanced at the shop, but I ducked behind a sack which hung from the ceiling.

'Can I help you, Miss?' the proprietor repeated. 'I'm closing up in a few minutes.'

'Thank you, no. I'll come back another day.'

I left the shop. The street was shutting up and the couple were nowhere to be seen. I was still at a loss. 'What would your father have done? What would your Mr Henry have done?' Henry would have gone to the police. I had done exactly the sort of hare-brained thing that Father would have done. Half prepared, half relying on luck. At least I could gauge a little of the area before catching an omnibus into London.

Around the church were a number of large houses, lit up for the evening. Upper rooms were dark or candlelit. What if 'Miss Holland' was trapped in one of those? Could she drop her letter and hope someone would pick it up and post it on her behalf? They were very high windows. And besides, if that was her house, someone would know she was there.

I walked into the churchyard, listening for footsteps, unnerved by the looming angels and spiked tombs. It was too dark to see; I would have to come back. But I could walk a little further.

Beyond the church was a row of tiny houses; in

comparison, my house was a mansion. The lamps were more sparse. It was not a slum by any means but nor was it well to do. Steps behind me made me turn. The familiar silhouettes of Jack Spratt and his wife were approaching. All I could do was press myself back against the wall. A door opened, and I was hauled into a house.

The door closed and a large hand pressed itself over my mouth.

'Shh.' A male voice.

'Mr King, whatever are you doing?' I twisted round and saw a woman in a limp dark dress standing in the middle of the chilly room. She looked appalled, her left arm reaching out to me. Her right arm, I noted, hung limp and twisted at her side, its fingers crushed.

I squirmed harder and kicked my captor, finally wrenching myself free. He made no attempt to grab me again, but put his finger to his lips.

It was the handsome man from the omnibus. In the dim candlelight, his expression was hard to read. His mouth was set firm and his eyes no longer smiled, but they seemed to hold warning rather than threat.

'What do you think you are doing?' Fear and fury competed and I started towards the door.

'Ma,' said a little voice, 'why is the lady so cross?'

I looked round. A thin child had appeared, hugging a rag-doll, and a scrawny boy of about fifteen.

The man bowed.

'I'm sorry,' he said to me, 'I didn't mean to frighten you. I can explain. Don't leave just yet, they are still likely to be outside.'

He turned to the woman, who stood holding the child against herself with her good arm.

65

'Maria,' he said, 'they're here. They've come to find you. And now they're after this young lady too.'

Chapter 10

Connie

'Ow!' I wanted to turn my head and glare at Mary, but I feared another burn if I moved.

'Sorry, Miss Connie,' Mary said, completely unrepentant, 'but if you will wriggle —'

'I didn't wriggle!'

'Well, try not to. I'm nearly finished.'

I sniffed the air, but mercifully the smell of singed hair was absent. Hopefully I would get through the ordeal of being prepared for dinner unscathed. Being prepared for dinner . . . that made it sound as if I was going to be on the menu. I imagined myself, party dress on, apple in mouth, with the butler scraping his carving knife and fork over me —

'Miss Connie!' Mary stood back, exasperated. 'How am I supposed to do your hair when you're sniggering like that?'

'Sorry, Mary,' I said, subsiding, and stared into the mirror while she curled and primped and pursed her lips over me.

I was almost looking forward to the Frobishers'. For one thing, Jemima had excused herself on the grounds of indisposition. While I didn't rejoice in my sister's illness — of course not — she was a frightful tattle-tale. Even Mother's eyes couldn't be everywhere, but if Jemima saw me slouching, or eating too much dessert, or not being good company — not talking enough, talking too much, refusing a dance, etc., etc. — Mother would be informed. Purely for my own good, you understand. 'You don't want a reputation as a bore, do you dear? Or a gossip? Or a glutton?'

'No, Mother,' I would say, red and fidgety, and wish myself anywhere but in her boudoir, being lectured. Again.

But tonight would be different. For one thing, Mother had been in excessively good spirits ever since I had mentioned that Mr Lamont would also be attending. I wasn't sure if that meant I would be more or less closely observed, but I hoped for the latter, so long as I wasn't doing anything outrageous. And when Mary had finished with me, and I was suitably gowned and bejewelled, I thought I looked almost pretty.

It was a half-hour drive to the Frobishers' house in Cheyne Walk. Mother took the opportunity to talk to me as if I were fourteen and disappointing. 'Don't slouch, don't eat too much, don't gawp, and make sure you seem interested when people are speaking to you. I hope there won't be a repeat of what happened at the Minivers'. Although you do look very nice tonight, dear.'

A footman ushered us into the drawing-room for pre-dinner drinks, and Lady Frobisher bustled to greet us, a cheery, stout presence in vermilion who reminded me, just a little, of an over-ripe tomato. 'Well now, Miss Connie, don't you look fine!' she exclaimed, clasping my hands.

My mother beamed, and I let myself bask in the glow for a moment. And then I caught sight of Albert, loitering by an aspidistra, and I felt the glow deepen to a burn. *Don't go red*, I willed myself. *It'll look even worse than usual because you're wearing blue.*

A waiter handed me a small glass of bright-green liquid which made me think of poison. I was tempted to down it but the thought of my mother's expression held me back. 'Thank you,' I said, and sipped.

My eyes met Albert's over the rim of the glass, and I froze. He smiled, and weaved his way through the knots of people until he was at my side. 'We meet again, Miss Swift,' he said, with a little bow.

'Indeed we do, Mr Lamont,' I said, giving him my hand. Albert was, as usual, beautifully dressed, in tailcoat and white tie with diamond studs.

I felt Mother quivering beside me, like an elegantly tailored pointer. 'Lady Frobisher,' she gabbled, 'would you indulge me in a private word?'

'Of course, my dear,' said Lady Frobisher, giving me an approving look, and encircling Mother's arm with her own dimpled one, led her away.

'You look suspicious, Connie,' Albert observed, finishing his drink and lifting another from a passing tray. 'And also very nice.'

'So do you, Albert.' Mother was talking to our host, their heads almost touching, and I caught a glance in our direction which was gone as quickly as I saw it. 'I think Mother's up to something.' Lady Frobisher lifted a finger, and a servant was at her side instantly.

'Isn't that what mothers do? Anyway, you can hardly complain about goings-on. I hope you haven't been mixed up in any more wild goose chases —'

'Shhhh!' I looked around wildly, but no-one was paying us any attention. They were far too busy with their own conversations. 'Don't talk about that here!' I muttered.

A gong sounded in the hall. 'Shall we?' said Albert, offering an arm. And when he took me into the dining-room, it turned out that he had been placed on my right.

***

'Caviar, ma'am?'

'Just a little, please,' I said, but the waiter's conception of just a little was different from mine. My heart sank at the mass of shining black oozing over my plate. I caught Mother's watching eye, and she nodded in approval.

I couldn't even commiserate with Albert. Lady Frobisher had chosen to start the conversation in the other direction, and I was required to chat with a bluff, hearty man with a moustache which would have looked over-large on a walrus, who introduced himself as Major Fairbank. 'Flummery,' he said, spooning his caviar onto a piece of toast and crunching it savagely. And that was all he said. I hoped Lady Frobisher would switch sides soon, but suspected I was stuck with the Major until the fish course.

A light touch on my right elbow made me jump. 'Excuse me,' said Albert. 'Would you mind if I pinched some of your caviar? I seem to have run out.'

'Be my guest,' I said, smiling politely, though inside I was grinning like the Cheshire Cat. I moved my plate to the right, and Albert helped himself to a generous spoonful, leaving — could it be? — exactly half.

70

'Thank you so much, Miss Swift,' he said, and turned back to his partner.

As I had predicted, Lady Frobisher turned at the fish course, and so did we all. 'You can't have any of my turbot,' I said, decisively.

'Wouldn't dream of asking,' said Albert. 'Funny, isn't it?'

'I'm sorry, what?'

He gestured with his fork at the table centrepiece. 'You begin looking for something, and you see it everywhere.' There, among the roses and syringa, were tall yellow tulips.

'No black tulips, though,' I commented.

'Black tulips?' bellowed the Major. 'What would anyone want with a black tulip?' The table fell silent for a moment, as everyone gazed at the source of the noise. Then the gentle hum resumed. I judged it best to ignore the Major's outburst, and hoped he would not pick the subject up when we turned again.

The rest of the meal passed without incident, and Albert gave me his ice to finish. 'A fair swap for the caviar,' he said. I glanced guiltily at Mother, but her expression signalled nothing but approval. I shrugged, and finished it. 'Now for ordeal by cigar,' sighed Albert, and I braced myself for coffee and chat with the ladies, and possibly a light grilling from Mother.

The gentlemen rejoined us relatively quickly. 'More time for dancing,' said Maisie Frobisher, rising to her feet. 'I told Mama we must have dancing.' I stifled my groan behind my hand, and looked for Albert.

He had somehow become invisible; but the Major strode over and was fastened to my arm in a moment. 'I'll take you in,' he snapped. 'I suppose you want to dance.'

'I —'

'Of course you do. That's what young ladies love to do, twirl round and make themselves giddy. Giddier than they already are. Come along.' The musicians in the gallery launched into a waltz, and off we went.

'What was all that rubbish about tulips?' the Major shouted in my ear, while I tried to keep my feet from being stamped on.

'Nothing,' I said, trying not to wince as he scored another direct hit. 'I saw some black ones in a painting, and wondered why you never see them in real life. Just a fancy, really.'

He snorted. 'A fancy, indeed.' We performed a few revolutions in silence, and then I caught sight of Albert, straight-backed, taking Maisie round. She looked very pleased with herself, while he looked as if he was counting in his head. I caught his eye, and for a second an expression of comical despair crossed his face.

Eventually the music stopped, and I curtsied to my partner. 'What's your name again?' he asked.

'Miss Swift. Do excuse me,' I said, and lived up to my name by fleeing. I couldn't face a second trampling.

I wandered into the orangery, which felt almost tropical with its lining of broad-leaved plants. I found a vacant seat and gazed around me, slipping my shoe off and flexing my poor abused toes.

'Would you like any refreshment?' A tall, fair young man in evening dress was standing before me. I put my shoe on hastily.

'Er, no, thank you. I am quite comfortable..' I assumed an expression which I hoped would convey that I wished to be left alone.

'I couldn't help overhearing' — he sat down in the nearest chair — 'what your neighbour was saying about black tulips, at dinner.'

'The Major? That was just a fancy,' I said firmly. Why was everyone I met so fascinated with tulips?

'Oh.' He shuffled his feet. 'My grandfather was obsessed with them.'

'Was he?' I said, trying to appear mildly interested rather than completely gripped.

'That's what Father says. Apparently he spent most of the family fortune on trying to cultivate a true black tulip, but nothing ever came of —'

'I think the next dance is mine, Miss Swift,' said Albert, smiling benevolently down on me. The young man stepped back, and I had no choice but to get up.

'Your timing is atrocious,' I hissed, as Albert led me to the floor. 'He was going to tell me about black tulips!'

'I thought I was doing you a favour,' Albert muttered. 'You looked awfully bored.'

'I was pretending! I didn't want to seem too eager.'

'Sorry,' said Albert, not sounding sorry at all. 'I was bored, anyway. I've danced the last three, and been told off, and giggled at. Dance this one with me, and then we can sit out for a while and gossip.'

'The last dance of the evening!' called the first violin. 'Take your partners for the last waltz!'

I grimaced. It would be a waltz, and I would have to submit to being spun round the floor by Albert, who had barged in on a promising conversation, and probably have my feet mangled again. But I had no choice. Mother was sitting on the sidelines. If I walked away from a gentleman

73

requesting a dance, I would never hear the end of it.

As it turned out, Albert wasn't such a bad dancer after all. We only trod on each other once apiece, and within a few bars I felt distinctly more cheerful. As evenings went, particularly social evenings, it had been a success. I had avoided the caviar, eaten extra dessert, and escaped direct censure from Mother. Now I just needed to find out the name of the fair young man.

The music scraped to a close, and when I rose from my curtsey Mother was at my side. 'Mr Lamont,' she purred. 'So nice to see you. Do feel free to call. Carriages, Connie, carriages.'

'Why are we rushing?' I asked, as Mother whisked me towards the cloakroom.

'Never mind,' she said. 'Go and get our things, dear.'

Maisie Frobisher was hovering by the door with her mother, bidding farewell to the guests; Lord Frobisher, as was usual on these occasions, had appeared only at dinner. 'Last dance with Mr Lamont, then?' she said.

'I didn't know it was the last dance,' I protested.

'Of course not.' She smirked.

'I didn't!'

'Goodbye, Connie.'

'Wait!' I leaned in closer. 'I was talking to a fair-haired young man earlier, but I didn't catch his name. Do you know who I mean?'

Maisie frowned. 'There are so many of them...'

I scanned the hall. There he was, in the doorway. 'That one,' I said, pointing.

'Oh,' Maisie peered. 'Oh, him. That's Toby Langlands. No-one to bother about.'

'Ah,' I said, 'thank you.'

'Connie!' Mother was tapping her foot.

'So why did you bundle me off like that?' I asked, as our carriage rattled down the empty streets.

'Do you really want to know?' she asked, her eyes wide and innocent.

'Yes.'

Mother smiled. 'I hurried you away because I don't want Mr Lamont to get tired of you.' She leaned forward and pressed my hand. 'You should always leave them wanting more, dear.'

I gasped.

'Oh, Connie,' she laughed. 'You are so silly.' And her merriment rang out as the carriage bowled on.

CHAPTER 11
Katherine

'Who?' I said, 'who's after me? And who are *you*?'

Mr King bent to rub his shin.

'Ever been the back end of a pantomime horse?' he asked. 'You're well qualified.'

'Lots of cousins to kick,' I said. 'Now if you'll excuse me.' I reached round him for the door handle. He stood up and held my arm.

'Let me out.'

'Wait.'

'Mr King, you're frightening her.' Maria came over.

'I'm James King,' he said, dropping my arm to rummage in a pocket for a card. 'You may have read my articles in the papers.'

I shook my head.

'I try to get comfortable people to read about the people who keep them comfortable, and what it's like to be poor.'

'I keep telling you, Mr King,' said Maria, standing tall

and sticking her chin out. 'My Reg will support us, won't you Reg?'

The lad grunted.

'I'm not asking for charity and it's my cold, dead body they'll have to take to the workhouse. We'll manage.'

'I'm sorry,' I said suddenly feeling overdressed and overfed, 'I really am, but I don't know why that led you to pull me in here, Mr King, and I'd like to leave.'

'I've been following two people who pose a threat to Maria. It's a long story.'

The woman stepped forward. 'You can trust him, Miss. He's been a friend to us. I thought no-one would help me after my old mistress died. If Mr King hadn't been asking questions around our lodgings, I'd never have known where to turn.'

'He got us this place,' burst out the boy. 'They can't put us in the workhouse if they can't find us.'

'Gart!' spat the woman. 'She never had an ounce of kindness in her.'

I had no idea who they meant. But it was no concern of mine.

Mr King turned to me. 'By chance I overheard those two on the omnibus talking about Maria and followed them. But they suddenly took a keen interest in you when you put down that dusty old book and started reading letters. I don't know what you have to do with any of this, Miss…'

'Black tulips,' I said.

'That's not a name,' he said.

I put my hand back on the handle and tried to stop it shaking. What if I opened it and someone was waiting?

'No, that's not my name,' I said, 'but it's what I'm

looking for.'

The boy snorted. 'Ain't no such thing as black tulips.'

'Isn't,' said Maria.

'Isn't no such thing as black tulips.'

Inasmuch as I could see in the dim candlelight, there was no reaction to the words. No wariness or tension. It was all a misunderstanding.

'I wish you well, Maria, and I wish I could help, but I can't. I'm leaving now,' I said and stepped outside.

The street was empty. Somewhere distant a dog barked and another answered.

'You can't let her walk alone,' I heard Maria say.

'I like my shins the shape they are.'

'Go on.'

Mr King caught up with me.

'What —' The rattle of wheels made us turn. A cab, moving briskly, came to a sudden stop. 'Not you again!' said the cabman. 'At least you picked a better neighbourhood this time.'

It was the one who'd chased Miss Armitage. Sam Webster.

'Do you know where this young lady lives?' said Mr King.

'Yus.'

'I suggest you take her home, it's getting late. It's not safe.' He turned to me. 'Have you...?'

I still had what was left of Albert's ten shillings. It must surely be enough. Much as I hated admitting it, Mr King was right. It was getting late and it probably wasn't safe.

'We're old friends,' said the cabbie, 'she'll have the right fare. Hop on, Miss.'

'You have my card,' said Mr King, helping me up the

step. 'I'm sure you won't be able to resist getting in touch. Most women can't.' He sprang away before I could kick him.

'Fog's coming dahn,' said the cabbie as we slipped through suburbs into London.

Fog, I thought. *She said it was foggy. She was writing from inside London proper. The postmark is irrelevant.*

I laid my head back and groaned.

When I got home, an anxious Aunt Alice and a letter were waiting. The letter was from Connie, sent that morning. She wanted to take me for tea after work tomorrow, since we only worked half a day on Saturdays. She wanted to talk things over properly. She said none of it made sense. I couldn't argue with that.

***

A display in the windows of Harrods made us stop.

Two mannequins dressed in the latest Paris fashions stood side by side in splendour. Full busts, broad hips, eighteen inch waists.

Connie and I both sighed at exactly the same time. My eyes refocused on my reflection and then realised Connie was doing the same with hers. Our eyes met in the glass. There was nothing average about either of us.

'At least you could manage the waist,' said Connie, 'I'd need to remove half of my ribs.'

'Yes but I'd need a million pillows to give me a bust like that. In fact, I could do with one to give me any sort of bust.'

'True, and if you tried to walk in a skirt like that, you'd fall flat on your face.'

'At least I wouldn't be a hussy. From the pavement I'd have a wonderful view of your ankles and half your shins if you were wearing a skirt that length.'

'What a pair. We're so odd.'

'Unique you mean. Unique.'

Connie laughed. I joined in, imagining the two of us capering around in ill-fitting clothes. A passing lady tutted. She paused to murmur: '"Her voice was ever soft, gentle and low; an excellent thing in woman". No gentleman likes a hoyden, girls. No lady draws attention to herself. You both look too refined to be shrieking like steam trains.' She squinted closer at Connie. 'Don't I know your mother?' She rummaged in her bag and pulled out a lorgnette.

'I don't think so,' said Connie, grabbing my arm and leading us away.

'Ladies never hurry either,' I pointed out as we scurried along the pavement.

'Well, even a galleon has to speed up occasionally.'

'Galleon?'

'It's what my mother calls me.'

'How rude,' I said before I could stop myself.

'If I'm a galleon,' said Connie, leading us into a tea-shop, 'that makes you a sort of tug boat. Although a tug is tubby and you're rather skinny, so perhaps you're more of a canoe. A skiff would be too long.'

I giggled, scandalising another set of old ladies.

'How may I help you?' We jumped as the waitress proffered a menu.

Connie didn't look. 'Full afternoon tea,' she said, 'no stinting on the cake. My friend needs building up into a more substantial vessel.'

We both started laughing again. Then, with the waitress gone, we subsided into silence.

Connie fiddled with her napkin ring. 'Katherine,' she

said, 'do you mind my asking about . . . well, about your family. I mean your cousin Albert is…'

'Not bad looking, nice, cleverer than he makes out?'

'Are you in love with him?' Connie burst out.

I snorted, earning myself a scandalised look from the waitress, who had appeared with a trolley bearing an entire patisserie.

'Hardly. He's like the brother I never had. But he's always been in the shadow of his elder brothers whom Ada describes as, let me get this right, "total ar . . . army material".'

The waitress, balancing the cake stand on the table, sniggered.

'I don't quite…' said Connie.

'I'll explain later. Albert is lovely, but don't tell him I said so. I'd just like to see him with a woman who appreciates him for what he is.'

'Yes,' she said, 'he does seem pleasant.'

I restrained myself from rolling my eyes. Was she blind? Albert was head over heels in love with her and he'd only met her twice.

'I hope you don't mind my asking,' she started. I primed myself to fight Albert's corner but she continued, 'he's your cousin? First? Second? Distant?'

'First,' I said. 'His mother was my father's older sister. She died when he was born, he's sort of runt of the litter.'

'He's pretty tall for a runt.'

'The others are built like outhouses. Except maybe Maurice junior. He's just tall and solid.'

'Oh. So you're very close…' She blushed.

'He's like my brother. I wasn't so close to the others because they're much older, but Albert and I sort of grew up together. His mother died when he was born and my mother did her best to step in, rather than leave him to nursemaids.'

Banging on the window made us look up.

'Away with you!' cried the waitress, hurrying to the window. The whole room turned and saw a grubby, ragged, scrawny child slink off. Dirty marks streaked the windows where he'd peered in.

'Those paupers should be in the workhouse,' murmured the woman next to me, 'troubling decent people like this, it's appalling. He ought to be birched.'

'Poor child,' I said, 'I'm sure it must be awful being hungry and watching us having a treat just for fun.'

'Yes,' said Connie, 'I suppose it must.'

'I wonder whether that Mr King really does write about the poor.' I caught Connie's surprised look and reverted to Albert. 'The Lamonts are very kind. We haven't been . . . free to go to any dinners or dances at their house for a while, but Albert is still like my brother. He's kept an eye on things since Father has been — away, always willing when we need a male escort, that sort of thing. I expect it makes his life less dull. But I don't . . . I'd rather not be dependent. Miss Robson says that working women should be respected and I should be proud of myself,' I said.

'I think she's right,' said Connie, 'I wish I felt more useful.'

I sat and crumbled the cake on my plate, wishing I could take some home for the others. I had never spoken of our circumstances to anyone and here was Connie, richer than I'd ever been, with her own maid and coachman. I felt more tired than proud. As long as I didn't start to cry.

'Our families go back a long way. They came from

France in 1680. We were called de Meret or de Marais, and we were silk weavers.'

'How interesting.'

I looked up to see if she was being facetious, but her face showed fascination.

'Our family did well and the Lamonts — La Mont — did better. The businesses are long sold and inheritances invested so no one has . . . had to go out and earn a living. But to be honest, we were all right. We wanted for nothing. If Father had been a better investor perhaps we'd have been richer, but we were perfectly comfortable. And then Father became famous for his books.'

'They are very exciting.'

'I expect you were being prepared for coming out when his last one was published.'

'Probably. I did feel like a prize cow.'

I laughed but kept crumbling the cake.

'I wasn't grand enough to be presented but to be honest, I'd rather have gone to university.'

'But girls…'

'Exactly. Anyway, it didn't matter. Albert's father became Father's patron and paid for trips abroad so that he could write more books.'

'I'm surprised your father didn't take you. You seem so capable.'

'He had Henry. Henry is wonderful. So organised and calm.'

'Oh,' said Connie, 'that's who Henry is.'

I glanced up, and she looked down for a moment. 'Albert mentioned him,' she said. 'Were you engaged?'

'We have a sort of understanding.' I paused, then decided I might as well carry on. 'Three years ago, they went to Anatolia and never came back.'

'How awful.'

'Yes. But unless Father is proved to be dead, we have no income. He gave me a little sum to keep us for the year he expected to be gone, but didn't think to trust me with more. He still thinks I'm a child, really. And if Father is . . . I mean, we could, we have…' I swallowed, 'obtained small sums against an inheritance.'

Connie's hand crept across the table and touched mine.

'And Albert's father is kind. He is paying for Margaret's school fees. I was determined she would not leave school. Then Aunt Alice had an old friend who needed lodging and I . . . I found a job in an office. Women — according to the Postmaster General — "have small fingers and are ideally suited to typing". We are also cheaper to employ.'

Connie said nothing. I kept staring at the crumbs. After a while she said, 'I can't imagine how you did it.'

'There was no one else. Besides, I'm sure we'll hear from Father and Henry soon.'

'That's the spirit,' said Connie. 'By the way, your cake is dead. Perhaps you could try to demolish a mini eclair in the usual manner of eating it?'

I took a cheese puff instead and opened my handbag, pulling out the two letters and spreading them on the table.

'To business,' I said, 'unless you want to talk about Albert again.'

'No thanks,' said Connie, looking away. 'Mother is already choosing bridesmaids. I don't need you joining in.'

'Mmm,' I said.

A shadow over the letters indicated the waitress had reappeared. 'More tea, ladies?'

'Yes please,' said Connie, still reading. 'Could we have a pot of Assam this time? Something you can get your teeth into.' The waitress withdrew. 'Do you think...' she said.

'Do I think what?'

'Do you think this might be nonsense? Or the writings of a lunatic?'

I picked up the first letter and reread it. That agitated handwriting, the blots and crossings-out. The lack of a name. 'I did wonder,' I said.

'Perhaps we should take them to the police.'

'That's what Henry would do.'

'And your Father?'

'Oh he'd try to do what we're doing, only without being hampered by work, aunts, mothers and long skirts.'

'So what should we do?' said Connie. 'I can't bear to think of a poor woman in danger but equally, I'm worried that we are putting ourselves in danger for a madwoman. Person. We don't even know it's a woman.'

That was true.

The waitress returned with the fresh pot of tea, and I told Connie about the previous evening.

She groaned. 'And all I had was caviar and the Major's feet.'

'I'd have changed places with you.'

'I think we should go to the police.' She picked up a petit four and popped it into her mouth just as another bang resounded from the window. The child was back.

The waitress hurried through the gap between our table and our neighbour's, muttering.

'Really,' said the lady next to us, rising. 'I thought this was a respectable tea-shop.' She put some coins on the table and left, followed by several other people pushing past, while we watched the waitress haul the boy off by the ear. He was grinning as they disappeared out of sight.

'I hope she hands him to a policeman,' said someone else. 'That'll wipe the smirk off his face.'

The excitement over, I poured the tea.

We sipped in silence for a while, taking it in turns to read the letters and examine the envelopes. I pulled out another of Father's old books which I'd thought might help. This was one about physic gardens, or rather physick gardens. The heavy print seemed more indecipherable than before, the serifs and twiddles swirling and merging until the whole page was a whirling sea of black ink.

'Come on Miss, come on.' The waitress was slapping my cheek. The world was sideways. I could see chair legs and skirts and broken china and scattered cakes and carpet and Connie lying on the floor alongside me with someone slapping her too. A desperate urge to vomit came over me.

'Steady Miss, steady.'

I swallowed the nausea and tried to sit up.

'Careful now, don't sit up too fast, we've got a doctor coming.'

'My friend…'

'She's coming round, Miss.'

'My things…'

I struggled to get up.

'It's all right Miss, don't worry. Here's your bag and your purse and your book.'

I relaxed and started to lie down. Then I remembered.

'The letters? What about my letters? They were on the table.'

The waitress paused.

'No letters, Miss. I expect you'd already posted them. Now don't worry. The doctor's come. Just lie back down, Miss. Everything is all right.'

CHAPTER 12
Connie

I awoke, nauseous and dizzy, and found myself on a hard floor. 'What happened?' I murmured.

'We've been drugged,' groaned Katherine. 'And the letters have been taken.'

'Oh no.' My head swam as I sat up. I tried to focus, but all I could see were concerned faces, gawping at me and Katherine.

'Here's the doctor,' called the waitress from the door. She must have been watching for him, eager to get us off the premises and back to normal.

'What's happened here?' he asked, pushing his way through the tables. He had a bristling moustache and a brisk air about him.

'I think we've been poisoned,' said Katherine, and the waitress shot her a piteous look.

'Mm,' was all the doctor said, kneeling beside her and reaching for her wrist. 'Your pulse is slightly elevated,' he said, 'but that could be down to excitement. Look at me, please. Ah, your pupils are dilated. And from the mess around you, you had been taking refreshment when the malady struck.'

'Yes, both of us,' said Katherine. 'I think it was the tea. I was fine, and then suddenly I felt faint, and — that was it.' She set her jaw. 'I want someone to call a policeman. Some letters which were on the table have been stolen.'

The doctor said nothing, but came to examine me. 'The same symptoms,' he said. 'The chances of that happening without an incident of some kind are most unlikely. Now, do you think you can sit on a chair?'

'They can sit in our back room, doctor,' the waitress interjected, wringing her hands.

He considered. 'That might be better. But I shall take samples of the remaining food and drink, and send them for analysis. I suspect foul play.'

'Oh, sir!'

'Yes, sir,' he snapped. 'Now go and fetch a policeman. I'm surprised you haven't already.'

We were supported into the back room, with two staff on either side of us, and lowered into chairs. 'I don't want a policeman,' I said, under my breath. 'If my name is in the papers, Mother will kill me, never mind whoever tried to poison us.'

'But don't you see?' said Katherine. 'This is too big for us. We should hand it over to the police. We can't do this alone.' She looked smaller than ever, and very weary. Even her auburn hair looked subdued.

'Fine,' I said. 'We'll hand it over. But I'm giving a false name. I can't risk it.'

The doctor stuck his head round the door. 'How are you ladies getting on?' He eyed us. 'You seem to be doing well, but I'd recommend getting someone to take you home. You shouldn't travel alone.' He patted his bag. 'I've collected samples, and I've given my details to the policeman. We shall see.'

'Thank you so much,' I said. 'You've been very kind.' I reached for my bag.

'No, no,' he said, waving a hand. 'I shall send my bill to the restaurant. It's the least they can do.'

'So where are these ladies?' The loud voice was followed by a tall, broad, helmeted shape in the doorway. 'Had a funny turn, have we?'

'It was a little more than that,' Katherine said, quietly.

'Laced yourselves too tight, I expect.' The policeman winked at the doctor, who responded with a look of contempt. 'Suit yourself,' he said, and advanced, pulling out a notebook.

'I'll be on my way, then, constable,' said the doctor. 'Ladies, I wish you a speedy recovery.' He raised his hat, and departed, and suddenly I felt very alone.

The policeman fetched a chair, placed it before us, and sat down. 'Right,' he said, opening the notebook and taking out a pencil. 'Names.'

'Miss Fleet,' I said, hastily. 'And this is Miss Caster.' I didn't dare to look at Katherine.

He repeated the names, writing laboriously. 'Today's date, the fourteenth. Time,' — he consulted his watch — 'thirty-five minutes past four in the afternoon. There.' He scratched at the stubble on his chin. 'And what do you ladies wish to report?'

'We were drugged,' said Katherine, 'and someone took two letters.'

'Drugged,' he said, writing busily. 'Two letters.' He

looked up. 'Any money in the letters? Postal orders?'

'No,' said Katherine.

'And what makes you think you were drugged?'

'We both fell unconscious at the same time,' said Katherine. 'That's hardly normal.'

'Nothing else taken?'

We both rooted through our bags. As far as I could tell, everything was in order. 'Nothing from me,' I said.

'Or me — no, wait!' said Katherine. 'Someone gave me a card yesterday, and that's gone too.'

'So nothing of value.' The policeman closed his book. 'To be honest, ladies, there isn't much I can do. The doctor's done his bit, and now we have to wait and see. Maybe the cream had gone off in one of your cakes. That sometimes happens,' he said, meditatively.

'It was the tea!' I cried. 'I know it was!'

'Now, how can tea go off?' the policeman said, his eyes twinkling.

'Someone put something in it!' Why wouldn't he understand? 'You should go and talk to the kitchen staff, and see if they saw anything unusual, or if a stranger got into the kitchen, or —'

'Are you telling me how to do my job, miss?' His voice had gone from jocular to stern in an instant.

I bit my lip. 'No, constable, not at all.'

'Good.' He stood up.

'What happens now?' asked Katherine.

'I'll file a report at the station,' said the policeman, putting his notebook away, 'and then we'll see. Good day to you, ladies.'

When he had gone, we looked at each other. 'Miss Caster?' said Katherine.

'It was all I could think of,' I said miserably. 'You know, like the sugar.' I shifted in my chair. 'Still want to hand this over to the police?'

Katherine's glare could have melted iron. 'Don't be ridiculous.'

***

'Where do we go from here?' I asked no-one in particular, as the carriage proceeded in a leisurely manner down Pall Mall.

'To my house,' said Katherine, decisively. 'We need to talk.' She looked at Albert, who was fidgeting opposite me. 'If you don't mind, that is.'

'Well yes, actually, I do,' he burst out. 'You could have been killed!'

'That's a good point,' said Katherine. 'Whoever it was could easily have killed us, but they chose to knock us out instead. Maybe they're not properly villainous.'

'Not properly villainous!' snorted Albert. 'When will you learn, K? And you've dragged Connie into it, too.'

That stung me into speech. 'I haven't been dragged into anything!' I cried. 'I'm just as involved as she is! And I'm not giving up because some idiot drugged my tea — I'm going to track them down!'

Albert sighed, and pinched the bridge of his nose. 'And I suppose I have to chaperone you both round town like a tame nursemaid while you do it.'

'You don't have to if you'd rather not,' I said. A mean little imp was stirring within, whispering about Mother's plans for me. 'I'll just have to get in trouble. Or lie, and then get in trouble.'

Albert looked completely taken aback. 'But I thought —'

'What?' I snapped.

'It doesn't matter.' He sat back, and gazed out of the window.

'We're both tired, Albert,' said Katherine softly. 'It's been a long day. We're probably still feeling the effect of whatever it was they put in the tea.'

'Yes.' His voice was flat. 'I'll drop you at your house, and then I'd better go. I have a dinner engagement.'

'You always have a dinner engagement,' said Katherine.

He smiled, but it wasn't a smile I'd seen before. There was no amusement in it at all. 'Yes,' he said. 'I generally do.' His eyes settled on me for a moment, and then his gaze returned to the scene outside. His profile was clear and sharp against the darkening city; the high forehead, the long, straight nose, the full lower lip —

A sharp elbow dug me in the ribs, and I suppressed an exclamation. 'What?' I said, rubbing my side.

'Oh, sorry,' said Katherine, raising her eyebrows. 'My elbow slipped.'

Eventually we got to Katherine's, and Albert helped us out. I kept my eyes down as I gave him my gloved hand, and when I turned to say goodbye he was already vanishing into the carriage. 'Drive on,' he said, and clattered away.

'What a mess,' said Katherine.

'I know.' My head was spinning, I felt ill, and I wanted to cry. 'I was all right till you poked me in the carriage.'

'No you weren't,' she said, rummaging for her key. 'I poked you because you were staring at Albert.'

'Oh.' A sob came out of nowhere, then another, and I buried my face in my hands. Twenty-four hours ago I had

93

been having such a pleasant evening with Albert, and now he'd abandoned me on the pavement and gone off for another lovely dinner, where no doubt more women would dance with him —

'Shhh, shhh.' Katherine opened the door and bundled me in. 'Have your cry, and then go home. It's too late to do anything now.'

'I know!' I wailed.

She put her arms round me. 'Ohh.'

'What?'

'Never mind. I'm sure it will be much clearer in the morning.'

'I doubt it,' I sniffled.

Katherine didn't say anything to Aunt Alice about what had happened that day, blaming my tear-streaked face on weariness. She took me up to her bedroom, and helped me wash my face and restore my appearance to something like normal. 'I'll ask Ada to find you a cab,' she said. 'You need a good night's sleep.'

But when I got home there was no chance of sneaking upstairs for a nap. Mother was hovering. 'I wondered when you would return,' she said. 'A parcel came for you.'

'A parcel?' My brain felt fuzzy, as if it needed spectacles.

'Yes dear, a parcel.' Mother indicated the card tray on the hall table, on which now stood a small cube wrapped in brown paper. *To Miss Swift*, said the neatly-printed label.

Who would send a parcel to me? It wasn't my birthday, and I couldn't think of anyone who would send me a random gift.

'Well, open it, then!' Mother was fizzing with excitement.

I slid my finger under the sealing-wax, and lifted one flap, then another. The brown paper unfolded to reveal a small wooden box, inside which curled a dark, dark purple tulip. With it was a visiting card, on which the same neat hand had written *Almost, but not quite.* I turned it over.

It was Major Fairbank's card.

Chapter 13
Katherine

Aunt Alice insisted I stayed in bed till noon on Sunday. Connie had suggested I come round for Sunday afternoon tea, but Aunt Alice vetoed it; firstly on the grounds that we both needed to recover, and secondly that gadding about on Sunday was improper. If I was too unwell to go to church, then I was too unwell to go visiting. Neither of us had the energy to argue. The thought of tea made us both feel queasy, and if I looked as she did and she felt as I did, there was little we could achieve.

Nevertheless, Connie sent a note via Hodgkins at noon hoping I was better and asking when we could meet again. I sent one in return asking if she would like to come to dinner on Tuesday, wondering, as soon as it was too late to change the message, what on earth we could provide which would impress her.

After a lunch of beef tea, I was allowed to come downstairs in my wrap and lie on the drawing room sofa.

'I really don't think you should go to the office tomorrow,' said Aunt Alice, as if I owned it and could pick and choose the days I attended on a whim. She was stitching at something blue. Margaret slouched in an armchair with a book, kicking the hearth. Aunt Alice didn't approve of card games on Sundays and it was hard to imagine anyone looking more bored.

'I'll be fine tomorrow,' I said. 'Besides, I can't cover the loss of another day's pay, and since I took a day's leave at short notice, I would be very unpopular.'

Aunt Alice made an odd noise, and put down her sewing to dab at her eyes with her handkerchief.

'I do so wish I could be more help,' she said. 'Perhaps I should take a bit from my savings.'

I tried to sit up, failed and glared at Margaret, willing her to have a little sensitivity and hug our aunt. She ignored me.

'Don't be silly,' I said as gently as I could. 'It provides your only income and you put your fair share in to the household. Miss Charles isn't unreasonable. I'll explain that I was taken ill on Saturday and she'll keep my workload as light as she can.'

'You'll take the omnibus though, won't you?'

I couldn't afford the omnibus. All my spare money and Albert's loan were gone, but Aunt Alice needn't know. I changed the subject.

'What are you sewing?'

'Oh, I er… My grandmother always disapproved of sewing on the Sabbath,' she said, and bundled it away. I hadn't the energy to argue.

I must have dozed. When the door-bell rang, it was four o'clock. Half asleep, a thousand thoughts went through my mind.

It's Father. It's Henry. It's Connie. It's Miss Armitage. It's Jack Spratt. It's Mr King.

It was Albert.

'How do K,' he said, and wedged himself into the chair Connie had sat on just a few days ago, the day we first met.

'You look frightful,' he said.

'Thanks. So do you,' I retorted. It was true, I had never seen him so down in the mouth. He really had it badly. I didn't have the energy for this either.

'Are you sure you're visiting the right woman?' I asked.

Aunt Alice looked startled, and Albert blushed.

'You're the only one who'd welcome me,' he said. Aunt Alice brightened. Once, she'd held what she thought was a secret desire for us to make a match of it.

'Honestly Albert,' I said, 'you are exasperating. Go and visit. Just not today.'

'Is today a bad day?'

'Oh please don't tell me you tried. I mean, look at me. I'm hardly at my best. Do you think she'll receive visitors?'

'I don't care what she looks like. I just wanted to know she was recovering.'

He sighed. Aunt Alice subsided with a sigh of her own.

'Anyway, I brought some magazines for you. Lots of pictures. Suitable for girls . . . I mean convalescents.'

He handed over *The Tatler*, *The Lady* and the *Illustrated Police News*. I hid the last one before Aunt Alice saw.

'Would you care for tea, Albert?' she asked. Nausea nearly overwhelmed me and I closed my eyes. The next time I awoke he was gone and I was being chivvied back to bed.

***

I had hoped the walk to work on Monday would revive me. The morning was beautiful with frost, and even the sooty walls looked as if they were studded with diamonds. But the pavement felt cold and hard through my thin shoes, and the air bit through my winter coat. My mind was full of two nights of strange dreams; swirling faces and symbols, letters and books and paintings. I felt as if the events of last week were part of those dreams. They'd seemed real enough at the time, but were now as insubstantial as a spike of frost on a blade of grass.

My bag felt heavy on my shoulder even though it only held my purse. By the time I arrived at the Department I was exhausted. And we would never know what had poisoned us since Connie had given false names. Caster indeed. At least it was sugar not oil which had come to her mind.

I explained to Miss Charles that I had been unwell and she was sympathetic but distracted. One of the messenger boys had resigned and there were insufficient to go round. Naturally our team was the one who lost out, and yet people complained that our work was slow. The morning dragged. Miss Charles was irritable. I felt clammy and weak.

At lunch I went to the library to read the papers. Nothing about our experience had been reported, which was perhaps unsurprising; the tea shop had doubtless made sure that it was not. I flicked through the personal advertisements but nothing resonated. In the letters, there was a complaint about interference by 'so-called journalists' with sentimental sensationalist views.

Sir, the very foundation of our society is that hard work, temperance and discipline will reap their own rewards. There is no place in a civilised country for layabouts and work-shy whiners. Why should the decent industrious citizen concern himself with the miseries the idle bring upon themselves? At great public expense, the state provides workhouses for the destitute. It is quite right that these are not places of pleasurable rest, while the righteous poor labour to provide for their families. Yet journalists such as Mr King would have us believe that people are being treated unfairly and unjustly, and that their inability to put food on the table for their (almost always) excessively large brood is down to misfortune not imprudence. This is akin to rewarding idleness and punishing thrift. I am staggered that your eminent publication gave him as much as a sentence on Friday to broadcast his impious views…

It went on in this vein for some time.

I paused and rummaged in my handbag. Of course, his card was gone. I remembered his impudent face and his hand on my mouth. Firm and yet gentle. I felt my face become hot. And yet he seemed genuinely to care about the woman Maria with her ruined arm.

I could work. What could she do? All she had was Reg to make a living for them.

In the last few minutes of my lunch hour, I drafted a letter to Mr King care of *The Times*.

Dear Mr King, your heart appears to be in the right place. You might know of a family who needs help. Perhaps with only a young boy to provide for his mother and little sister. A vacancy for a messenger boy has arisen in The Department. I don't know how feasible this would be for him, or how appropriate, but it is all I can do to help. Yours —

What would I call myself? I wanted as little to do with the man as possible.

I signed it '*D*' and left it at that, posting the letter as I returned to work.

***

When I got home Aunt Alice handed me a note from Connie.

Mother insists I go to the seaside to recuperate and "keep out of mischief". She blames me for making you ill and doesn't wish me to look pallid for any "visitors". On the other hand, she's hoping the sickness will make me lose weight. I shall do my best to avoid this. I return on Saturday but hope to write to you while away, as I have something to ask your advice on. Do you think floral designs will be in fashion next season? Especially in black. It is a <u>Major</u> problem. I have information to this effect. I hope you are on the road to recovery. Best wishes to you and <u>all</u> your family.

There was also a note from Albert. *K, can you find out what I've done wrong?*

I wished they would both do their own investigations and leave me in peace.

***

The week dragged. I dreamed of crashing waves and sea air. I spent my evenings in Father's study, going through his books. On Thursday, I looked through the drawers in his desk and in one, found an old photograph. I smiled, remembering the day it was taken, here in this very study. Father was sitting at his desk and next to him was a small blur which was me, unable to stand still. He had not framed it because of the blur. I compared the photograph and the room, thinking how little the study had changed, and how much everything else had.

I frowned at the photograph and then at the room. I got up, stood where the photographer had stood, and looked again. Putting the photograph down, I went over to an innocuous print of an insipid girl in Grecian pose and took it down. A faint rectangle showed where the picture had protected the wall from the sooty air; but within it was a smaller square of untainted wallpaper. A smaller picture had once been in this place. I tried to recall it.

'Oh,' said Aunt Alice, when I took the photograph through to the drawing room, 'I hoped you'd never find out. I am sorry. It was deceitful of me.'

'What was?'

'Your mother always hated that picture. She begged me to hide it and got another to take its place. I'm not sure your father noticed. I mean, he fussed a bit. But when your mother explained it was stored away, he didn't seem to mind. He preferred the rather under-clad young woman, I think.' She blushed.

'But what was the original picture?'

'It was a horrid grubby thing,' she said, 'I don't know where he'd obtained it. Flowers, in the Dutch style. Very unpleasant.'

'Where is it now?'

Aunt Alice looked contrite. 'One day when things were

very bad, a few months ago, and I wasn't sure there was enough to pay the doctor when Margaret was so poorly, I confess I sold it. I'm afraid I didn't sell it for very much. I'd never done that sort of thing before. But I felt too foolish to argue. And then we managed the fees anyway.'

'Oh. I see.'

She brightened again. 'But somehow, you bought it back. I have no idea how you managed to pick exactly the same one. I found it one day when I was tidying up.'

My heart stopped.

'It was exactly the same?'

'Well…' Aunt Alice looked vague. 'It was certainly as horrid and grubby. But you know those sorts of paintings. They all look the same.'

***

The man on the flea-market stall on Friday lunch-time was uninterested.

'Might've, might not've. I know some woman sold me a painting like that for thruppence. She had a look o' you and she was a bit taller'n you and her hair was sorta the same colour. But it wasn't as carroty.'

I bit back my retort. 'Was it the same one you sold to me for sixpence?'

He shrugged, then his eyes narrowed. 'Could be. Why? What's wrong wiv that? Gotta make a profit ain't I?'

There was nothing more to be said. I turned towards the office, trying to make sense of it all. I missed Connie. Her letters had not explained her cryptic message from Monday and I suspected 'Mother' was monitoring what she sent. As I turned a corner, someone stepped out and we collided.

'Hello,' said Mr King. 'I see you've taken to doing your investigations in daylight. Very wise.'

103

I blinked.

'Thanks for the tip about young Reg,' he continued. 'Maria found lodgings nearby and he's starting on Monday.'

'How did you know…'

'Ah, you forget that I am an investigator myself. It wasn't hard to work out who had written me the letter. Who else knew about Reg? And the only way you'd know about a job in the Department was if you worked there. All I had to do was lurk outside to confirm it really was you, and ask a few key questions. Miss Demeray, I can spot when someone else is investigating, and I suspect you need some tips.'

Chapter 14
Connie

If there's a place more dismal than Broadstairs out of season, I don't want to go there.

I had spent most of Sunday and Monday confined to bed, with Mary bringing up trays which were beautifully presented but mostly bare of food. 'I blame myself,' said Mother, on one of her visits to my room. 'Dinner at the Frobishers', and all that excitement, followed no doubt by too much cake the day after. I think you're liverish.'

'I'm quite well, Mother,' I said, but she regarded me through narrowed eyes, and shook her head.

'Your colour's too high, and you look — I don't know what exactly — but *not right*.' She peered at me again. 'Did you, by any chance, see Mr Lamont yesterday?' Her voice was as velvety as a cat's paw, and had the same promise of razor-sharpness.

I shifted in the bed, which had become uncomfortably warm. 'We ran into him briefly, yes.'

'It won't do,' said Mother, folding her arms. 'There is

no point in me trying to manage things between the pair of you if you run to him the minute my back is turned.'

'I didn't!' I cried, and suddenly I felt faint and weak. Was that what *he* thought?

Mother smiled. 'You just happened to run into each other. You and his cousin, Miss Demeray. I wasn't born yesterday, Constance.' She smoothed my covers, absentmindedly. 'Leave it to me.' And she swept out of the room.

I lay back on the pillows and tried to think. My head still felt heavy, and my thoughts were slower than usual and blurred at the edges. What had Katherine and I been given? If only I could have gone downstairs to the library, and spent some time with an encyclopaedia, I felt sure I could have worked it out. I watched the sun creep across my quilt, and thought of our letter-writer — Miss Holland, as she had become — and wondered what she was doing now. Would we receive another letter from her, or would whoever-it-was track her down? I remembered the looping, curling writing, the strange half-thoughts and crossings-out —

And then it struck me.

She seemed confused. I felt confused.

Perhaps, like Katherine and me, she had been drugged. Not once, but many times.

That, unlike so much else in this case, made sense.

I smacked the quilt in frustration. I had made a discovery, and there was no way of communicating it to Katherine! I had already had to censor a note to her, since when I asked for my letter-case Mother had sat next to me and openly read over my shoulder. When her reply had arrived, suggesting dinner, Mother had twitched it away.

'You two should keep apart for a while,' she said. 'You've probably given her whatever it is you've got already.'

'At least let me reply,' I pleaded.

'We'll see,' she said crisply.

And when Mother returned, it was with the news that we were travelling to Broadstairs for a rest cure. 'You can't get into mischief there,' she said. 'And it's off-season, so it will be lovely and quiet. Just sea air and tranquility.'

'Couldn't we go to Brighton?' I asked. 'It's got just as much sea air.'

'It has,' said my mother, pulling the curtains as wide open as they would go. 'It also has fashionable people wintering there. You are in no fit state to be seen, Constance. You look half-dazed.'

'That's because I'm bored,' I retorted.

'Nonsense,' she replied. 'A change is as good as a rest, and that is what I intend to provide. It won't be any fun for me either, you know.' She rang the bell for Mary. 'Pack for five days at the seaside, please. Don't worry about evening dresses, she won't need any of those.'

I sulked as Mary bustled round the room, folding shawls and dresses into my trunk. I didn't stop sulking when Father stooped through the doorway, though an appearance by my father at any event except mealtimes was a rare occurrence.

'Your mother, ah, tells me you're going away tomorrow,' he said, pulling at his moustache.

'It isn't my decision,' I said, flatly.

'Oh.' He looked nonplussed. 'Make sure you enjoy yourself, dear.'

'It's a rest cure, Papa. I'm there to do nothing.'

'That sounds nice,' he said, fiddling with his watch-chain. 'Well, I must get on.' And he ducked his way out. I had no idea what Father did, but it involved either being out at his office, or shut up in the study. Beyond that it was some sort of financial business, I was ignorant.

Broadstairs was even duller than I had thought. The beach, where we spent much of the day, was cold and windy, and the hotel was mostly deserted. Mother and I breakfasted in the large, echoing restaurant, and I was almost glad to take dinner in my room. The simple act of eating was unnaturally loud in that cavernous dining room.

Again, Mother had stood over me while I wrote to Katherine to explain my whereabouts. I could do no more than hint, and not very well at that.

I was stuck until Saturday. Stuck in my room, or stuck on an uncomfortable reclining chair in the bitter wind; it was all the same.

I hoped Katherine was feeling better and getting on with things, but at the same time I didn't care to think of her rushing about and taking omnibuses and solving the mystery without me. I felt in much the same trapped state as Miss Holland — and surely no captor could be more attentive, more vigilant than Mother. I couldn't write letters, she said, for it would tire me. And I received no letters. There were times when I wondered if she was actually trying to kill me through lack of stimulation.

However, all that meant was that my brain ran round and round the same track. What was Katherine doing? And, even worse, what was Albert doing? I remembered his smile-that-wasn't when Katherine spoke of his many dinner invitations, and how he had turned away —

'Whatever is the matter?' snapped Mother, and I realised that I was crying. Quietly, but crying.

I spent some time wiping my eyes, to try and come up with anything that wasn't the real reason. 'I'm so booooored!' I wailed. 'I have nothing to do!'

Mother clucked in exasperation. 'I'll go and find you some magazines. Just stop that noise.'

But the magazines had nothing in them to interest me. I flicked past the fashions — what did it matter? The stories were stupid, and I didn't care about any of the people, or whether they lived happily after. 'I've finished,' I announced.

Mother looked murderous, then rang for help. 'Is there a circulating library here?' she asked the boy.

'There is, ma'am.'

'Good.' She thought for a moment. 'Please ask someone to visit it and procure two or three books suitable for a young lady. Nothing too exciting.'

'Yes'm.' He took the note she offered, touched his cap, and vanished.

I spent the rest of our stay reading, and thinking. The books were a merciful escape from my prison, and I lived in Dickens's London and Charlotte Bronte's Villette quite happily, until I finished the stories and had to wait for more books. By chance, on the Thursday the pageboy brought a volume of Roderick Demeray's travel stories. I devoured them greedily, feasting on the detail, the different worlds, the strange people and customs. Where was he now, and what was he doing? He didn't seem like the kind of man to die. And what of Katherine's fiancé, Henry? I felt sure that there was much she had not shared with me.

In the spaces between books, or when the light was extinguished and I lay awake in the darkness, I thought of Albert, no doubt whisking another girl around the floor at that very moment, resplendent in evening dress. She would be pleasant and attentive, and laugh at all his jokes. She wouldn't snap at him, or be tongue-tied, or have a mother trying to push her at him.

I sniffed, and brushed a tear away before it reached the pillow.

Whatever happened, I still had Katherine. She was my friend, and we would solve the mystery together. As soon as I was back in London, I would tell her what I had learnt. And I would, somehow, find a way to travel and go out unchaperoned. Albert would, no doubt, accompany us if Katherine asked him to, through good manners and family obligation, but if he was going to flaunt his independence, I didn't want to see it. *Go to your dinners and dances, Albert*, I thought. *Chat to whomever you like. Just leave me alone.* I turned to face the wall, and sighed. One more day to endure. Then I would go home, and somehow — I didn't know how yet, but somehow — things would be different.

CHAPTER 15
Katherine

'Do you want my help or not, Miss Demeray?' asked Mr King. I wasn't sure if he was being genuine or teasing me.

Hesitating is not something I'm used to doing. It was hard to read Mr King's expression. His eyes were that peculiar hazel which change with the skies, one minute dark brown, another greenish. I shook myself.

'Do you think women aren't capable of working things out alone?' I said.

'On the contrary,' he replied. 'In my work I meet many women, and they are often very resourceful. I sometimes wonder whether the man who designated women as the weaker sex ever actually met one. But that's not to say that even a strong woman doesn't need help.'

'I'm not alone.'

I glanced at my watch and started to walk away. He followed.

'No, that's true,' he said. 'But you and your friend can

get into trouble simply by taking tea in the West End.'

I stopped and spun round, and he trod on my foot. 'I do beg your pardon.'

'How . . . what...?'

'A journalist has to make his bread and butter, you know. Trying to bring injustice into the public's gaze is neither simple nor lucrative. Nor is it welcome. I take on odd assignments to investigate to pay the bills. Emphasis on odd. Two ladies — one tall and well to do, another short and less so — collapse over the petits fours and macaroons and say the tea has been poisoned and their belongings stolen. Then they disappear under false names. Is it another instance of excuses made for tight-lacing?' He paused and perused me. I turned and walked off.

'Although,' he added, 'there's not enough of you to tight-lace unless you want to look like an egg timer. You're too short and slight to be an hour-glass.'

I flung my head up and walked faster.

'I suppose if I asked you to lunch with me you'd decline on the grounds of propriety,' he said, from about a foot behind me.

'I'd refuse on the grounds that I have two minutes to get to my desk and I am already in trouble at work as it is,' I threw over my shoulder.

We were nearly at the Department, but the road was busy with weaving carts and carriages. I prepared to chance it, and Mr King caught up with me. 'Then I'll wait on this corner at five and walk you home, and you can tell me what you're up to. If I can assist, I will. And maybe you can help me work out something plausible about the two mysterious tea-sippers.'

I stopped at the edge of the pavement and glared at him.

He put on a pitiful face like a puppy and then a serious face like an alderman.

'Not all the way home of course. I know what lurks behind the aspidistras in the windows.' He mimed curtain twitching. 'The genus *gossipa maliciosa*. Very prevalent in your street, I believe.'

I bit my lip to stop a grin. 'Maybe,' I said and dashed across the street, dancing between a cab and two bicycles and being sworn at by everyone.

'If it helps,' his voice came over the din as I scuttled up the steps, 'I went to school with Albert Lamont.'

***

'It's not fair,' said Margaret as she put her coat on after Sunday lunch. 'Why can't I stay and have tea with you and your friends?'

'Don't be such a misery,' I said. I reached over to pull her hair. 'Aren't you happy to be going out for a change?'

'Yes but I have to go with Aunt Alice. It'll be so boring.'

'What nonsense. One of your friends from school will be there.'

'Yes but I bet we won't be allowed to go and do anything interesting. And I'll be in the same old Sunday dress I've worn for a year and look at it. Aunt Alice has let the hem down three times. I look like a ragamuffin. I'm sick of being poor. All the other girls have nice things. Why can't I?'

'You know why. You should be glad you can go to school at all. I was taken out at fourteen so Father could educate me at home.'

'Yes but that didn't matter. There was money for trips and clothes. You had everything important.'

When she wasn't sulking Margaret looked so much like our mother that it made my heart hurt, but these last few months her face seemed to be in a permanent frown, except when she was with her classmates when she was just silly. I tried to remember if I'd been as bad at fifteen.

'Still, you'll have a nice tea,' I said. 'It'll be fancier than mine.'

She brightened. 'That's true, you've just Ada's cooking and not much of it. Aren't you embarrassed?'

'They'll have to lump it. Anyway, I made some little cakes myself. I'm quite proud of them.'

'That's even more embarrassing. When I grow up, I'm going to marry a rich man,' she said. 'I don't need an education or to learn housework.'

'I expect that's what Aunt Alice and Miss Robson thought too,' I said. 'Perhaps you should plan ahead in case it doesn't happen.'

'I'll never be an old maid like them or like you.' She forced her hat on and jammed in some hair-pins. Aunt Alice, reaching the foot of the stairs, fussed with Margaret's hat.

'Are you sure you'll be all right, dear?' she said. Her face was still troubled. I remembered James King's words as he'd walked me home. *How old are you? Isn't it time you made your own decisions about what you can and can't do in your own home?*

'All will be well, Aunt Alice,' I said. 'Connie, I mean Miss Swift, will bring her maid and Albert will chaperone us. Not to mention Miss Robson.'

'Yes but Miss Robson does tend to stay in her own room.' Aunt Alice's hands twisted.

'Aunt Alice, do stop worrying. We are not going to do

114

anything scandalous. Anyway, Ada would never allow it. She would beat the men out of the house with her broom.'

'Dead right I would,' said Ada, making us jump. 'I don't work my fingers to the bone in this house to have you mess it up with Shenanigans and I won't let Miss Kitty or Master Bertie give that Muriel at number nine anything to tattle about. Madam,' she said to Aunt Alice, 'you can rely on me to keep order.'

'I think Miss Swift has arrived,' I said. 'Have a lovely time.'

I hustled them out of the door as Connie and Mary ascended.

'Come along with me, young Mary,' said Ada. 'I expect you could do with putting your feet up. I'll take the young ladies tea shortly but I'm sure it won't kill them to wait.'

'Oh but...' started Mary as Ada dragged her towards the kitchen.

Connie and I looked at each other. I had a wild urge to hug her but settled for shaking her hand as usual. Then we both burst out laughing.

'I can't tell you how bored I've been,' said Connie. 'If ever I write to you again and tell you that Mother is taking me to the seaside, come and shoot me. I was reduced to reading improving literature. It was perfectly deadly. And if anything I'm now more rebellious than improved.'

'You could have given me your address and I'd have written. Or *someone* would have written.'

If she took my inference, she ignored it.

We sat in the drawing room and lounged. No mothers or aunts could tell us to sit upright, and we had half an hour before Albert would turn up. Or knowing Albert, possibly an hour.

115

'So what have you found out?' we said simultaneously. I continued, 'what on earth was all that about major floral dress decisions or whatever it was you wrote?'

'Ah.' Connie's smile drooped. She got up, went to the door and peered down the corridor, then she returned to her chair and pulled a card from her bag. She handed it over.

'This came with a tulip. The darkest tulip you've ever seen. I have no idea where you'd get tulips at this time of year but...'

'Is this the Major who stood on your feet at the dance?'

'I assume so. Or else it's someone using his name. I wouldn't know his handwriting.'

'Did he seem particularly threatening?'

'No. Just dull. Full of himself. A little...' she pulled a face as if vaguely revolted, 'he got rather close when we were dancing.'

I gave the card back. 'Anything else?'

'I managed to borrow one of your father's books from the lending library. I had forgotten how good they were.'

'Did it help at all? I've been looking through them too, but can't see any connection.'

'I have a feeling there's something, but I can't pinpoint it. Mother made it so difficult to concentrate, what with making a fuss and wondering if my book was too stimulating. But...'

'Yes?'

'I think "Miss Holland" must have been drugged. I mean, the way she wrote was how I felt all day Sunday. Just not quite right.'

Something finally made a little sense. 'Yes. That could be true.'

'And you?'

I told her about the painting. She groaned.

'I know, but I would never have remembered it in a million years. And I have no idea if it bears any significance whatsoever. There's something else.'

'Yes?'

At that moment Ada came in with the tea.

'Miss Swift,' she admonished, 'I don't know what you do to that young lass of yours, but she's worn out and fast asleep in front of the range.'

Connie looked contrite. 'I'm terribly sorry,' she said, ' I didn't know she was so tired.'

Ada tutted. 'Perhaps you should bring her more often.'

'I'd be glad to.'

Ada left, and we both listened till we were sure she'd gone. Then we looked at the tea tray. It seemed longer than a week since our outing.

'What else?' said Connie. 'There's something. I can tell.'

I poured out and spoke into the teacup, telling her about my letter to Mr King and the outcome, about his walking me home . . . almost all the way home. About telling him our suspicions, and why I had gone to Hendon.

'Why aren't you looking at me?' said Connie. 'My word, you're blushing.' She put her head on one side and contemplated me. 'How do you know you can trust him? Fancy telling a complete stranger all that.'

It was unusual to see her annoyed. 'He didn't seem like a stranger,' I retorted. Then I paused, and spoke more quietly. 'It's silly. But he didn't.'

'Mmm,' said Connie. 'But they can start off charming and then all of a sudden go cold on you.'

I blinked, finding it hard to believe she'd ever had much

experience with men. Now she was the one blushing.

'Well,' I said, 'I just have a feeling…'

'Like you did about the painting?'

'That's unfair. We were starting out then.'

We.

'Yes, we were. I'm sorry, that was unkind.'

I glanced at the clock. 'Oh and we have two other guests for tea,' I said.

At that moment a crashing noise came from the road. We both jumped up and went to the window. Outside were Albert and Mr King, tangled in what appeared to be a collection of scrap metal.

Connie gasped. 'What are they doing?'

'I have no idea,' I said. 'I mean, I invited them to tea.'

'Without your aunt?'

'I'm twenty-five,' I said. But I could feel my face forming into one of Aunt Alice's expressions as I imagined the neighbours peering out at the two gentlemen disentangling themselves from each other and what turned out to be two bicycles. 'And besides, Miss Robson is at home, and Ada won't put up with any Shenanigans. Here she comes now.'

Ada stormed down the hallway and opened the door as Albert made his way up the steps. His bicycle was propped against the railings. Mr King was about to follow suit.

'Master Bertie,' she said, 'you and your friend will take those contraptions round the back and put them in the yard. You will return properly once you have brushed the dirt from your clothes, and if you aren't clean, I won't let you in. I'm in two minds…'

'Steady on, Ada,' said Albert, 'I'm injured.'

'That's as maybe. You do as you're told, or you'll not

be having tea with two gentlewomen.' She slammed the door in his face and returned, muttering, to the kitchen.

Five minutes later, Albert and Mr King, dusted, stood at the door waiting admittance.

'I will bring fresh tea and the eatings,' said Ada, 'and you keep the door open, else I'll have the lot of you in the kitchen with me and Mary.'

The men hustled us into the drawing room before she could return.

'How do K, How do Con… Miss Swift,' said Albert. He looked miserable again. Connie reached out and shook his hand. I noticed she held it a second longer than politeness demanded. Albert's shoulders relaxed.

'Good day, Miss Demeray, Pleased to meet you, Miss Swift,' said Mr King, shaking hands quickly and checking the hallway. 'I just want to explain. The bicycles are my idea.'

'They saved a cab fare, I suppose,' I said, 'but you ought to learn to ride them properly.'

'They're not for us, they're for you. They're ladies' bicycles.'

Connie gawped. I gawped.

'Where did you get them?'

'Second-hand from two maiden ladies,' said Mr King. 'I talked your cousin into sharing the expense, Miss Demeray. You'll be better off with your own transport if you are going to roam about unescorted.'

'You're making those maiden ladies sound very delicate,' complained Albert, 'but they were, frankly, terrifying. The "votes for women" type. They are buying newer versions for more . . . whatever it is they plan to do.'

'Mother would never let me ride one,' said Connie,

wringing her hands. 'Even if I knew how.'

'I have to say,' said Albert, 'I do think they are inelegant. A lady's decorum should be maintained at all times.'

'Oh do shut up, Albert,' I said.

'Yes but you saw how easily we fell off, and we're wearing trousers,' argued Albert. His cheeks reddened and he stared at the ceiling. 'If you fell off, your legs might show.'

Connie started to laugh. 'We could always wear bloomers and long socks.'

I didn't think it was possible for Albert to blush harder, but he did.

'Anyway,' said Mr King, 'you can keep them here and practise when you have time and . . . er, freedom.'

'Hide them here you mean,' I said. 'Aunt Alice won't approve either.'

Mr King shrugged, then winked. 'You'll get round it,' he said.

Ada returned with the tea. It looked meagre compared to what Connie and Albert would be used to, and I felt silly. Whatever had I been thinking?

'What lovely scoff,' said Albert. 'I'm starving.'

Ada stood in the doorway as we ate and, after a few minutes of listening to Connie's innocuous description of her week in Broadstairs, left before she fell asleep.

'Thank goodness she's gone,' said Connie, 'I had run out of superlatives for the dullest holiday ever. I almost longed for another tea-shop incident to liven things up.'

'Ah,' said Mr King, 'the tea-shop incident. Now I can tell you what I've found out.'

CHAPTER 16
Connie

'Laudanum?' I felt sick all over again.

'That's what the doctor said.' Mr King stretched his long legs out in front of him. 'Apparently the cups were smashed on the floor when he arrived, but there was tea left in the pot. The lab said that even the dregs contained enough laudanum to put two people to sleep.'

'There,' I said triumphantly. 'I knew it was the tea.'

'Yes,' said Katherine. 'But how did laudanum get in the teapot?'

'Good question,' said Mr King. 'I had a word with the kitchen staff when I dropped in, and it looked very secure. No chance of someone nipping in by the back door and doctoring a pot of tea. And in any case, how would they know which one was yours?'

'Perhaps it was the waitress,' said Katherine. 'She'd know.'

'I don't think so,' I said. 'I'm sure she's worked there for some time.'

We pondered the problem, sipping our own tea. It was Albert who broke the silence. 'So if it wasn't the kitchen staff, and it wasn't the waitress, then it must have happened at the table.'

We all stared at him. 'It's the only logical explanation!' he said, reddening slightly.

'He's right,' said Mr King.

'It's possible,' I said thoughtfully, 'but we'd have seen them.'

'Not necessarily.' Mr King mused. 'Was there any kind of distraction in the room, do you recall?'

'Not particularly,' said Katherine. Then her face lit up. 'Yes! Not in the room, but — the boy at the window! The waitress went to shoo him away! It was about a minute . . . but that would have been enough.'

'There,' said Mr King. 'Can you remember how your table was set out? Where the teapot was?'

I frowned in recollection. 'The cake stand was in the middle, and the teapot . . . oh yes, when she brought fresh tea she put the pot on my left. I remember lifting it to pour out and wishing it was on the other side . . . actually that's odd...'

'What?'

'I remember now, someone went past, a thin woman in faded black not at all in fashion. She seemed to have trouble getting by and there wasn't much room, but she was quite narrow so she shouldn't have had too much difficulty. I thought she was a waitress because of the black dress, but now I think of it, she can't have been. It wasn't a uniform and she was wearing a hat, not a cap. She went by just as that boy came back and banged on the window. The ladies sitting next to us exclaimed and our waitress went outside. Do you remember, Katherine? And we both turned to watch her get rid of him. We must have been distracted for at least a minute.' What could I remember about the woman? I had seen so little of her... *Thin, of medium height, with a brisk, efficient gait* — I gasped. 'Miss Armitage!'

Mr King raised his eyebrows. 'All she'd need was a dropper filled with laudanum.'

'So we were followed,' Katherine said slowly.

'This won't do!' Albert exclaimed. 'You should turn it over to the police.'

'There's no point,' I said. 'We reported it, and look what happened.'

Katherine shivered. 'It's an odd thought that someone was watching us all the time, listening in, and we never knew. And now they have the letters.'

'Yes, but we're not finished with this,' I said. 'And we'll be harder to follow now, on bicycles.'

Albert's eyebrows shot up. 'I thought you couldn't ride one,' he said, quickly.

'I can ride a horse,' I said. 'It can't be that different.'

Mr King laughed. 'We have a convert. And you're right about the police. From what you've told me, they wouldn't touch the case. You'd just be dismissed as a pair of fanciful women.'

'Typical,' I muttered, taking another sandwich.

'All right then.' Albert sat up. 'You're not going to tell the police. But what are you going to do?'

'Investigate,' Katherine and I said, together.

'On bicycles,' I added, and Katherine snorted.

'But you don't have the letters any more,' said Albert.

'I don't think we need them,' said Katherine,

123

thoughtfully. 'We know the first letter was posted in Hendon, but the letter-writer — Miss Holland, we're calling her — can't have been that far out. She must be in London, because she mentioned the fog. She's being kept prisoner by the Magpie and the Viper. And Miss Armitage came to see me about the black tulips when I was expecting Miss Holland.'

'But the first letter was addressed to your father, wasn't it?' asked Mr King.

'That's right,' said Katherine. 'At first I didn't think anything of it. Father used to get all sorts of odd letters from his readers. Ideas for books, requests for help...' She smiled, and suddenly I could see how much she missed her father, and her old life. 'But now, there's the painting.' She told the story of the tulip painting which had gone backwards and forwards so many times, and I saw Mr King's eyes gleam. But when I looked at Albert, he was studying the carpet and chewing at his lower lip.

'Albert,' I said sternly, 'have you got something to say?'

Slowly, he raised his head, looking exactly like a guilty schoolboy. 'I'd forgotten it until now. It was something Father said, K, just after your father and Henry left for Anatolia. I was on the carpet in the study — I'd overspent myself — and Father was muttering about cash. He had a letter open on the desk, and I recognised your father's writing. I got a proper dressing-down, and then Father said "I've got enough shiftless relatives squandering my money without you adding to the number. Taking a diversion to look for tulips, indeed." And he screwed up the letter and threw it in the fire.'

Katherine stared at him, and her face crumpled. I

reached her as she began to cry, and put my arms around her.

'I'm sorry, K,' said Albert, looking utterly woebegone.

'I'm sure you are,' I said, 'but can you two make yourselves scarce?'

Mr King rose immediately. 'Of course. I'll be in touch,' he said. 'I have a feeling there's a lot more to this. Don't worry, I'll see myself out. Wait —' He reached into his pocket and put two cards on the mantelpiece. 'One for each of you. Try to keep hold of them this time.'

'Sorry. Again,' muttered Albert, and followed before I had a chance to reply.

Katherine's sobs were easing a little. I patted her back. 'It's all right,' I said. 'Take your time.' I felt her nod on my shoulder, which was now slightly damp.

Eventually she detached herself gently, rummaging for her handkerchief. 'Sorry I cried all over you, Connie,' she said.

'I wish people would stop saying sorry. Not you,' I said, as I caught her slightly hurt look. '*Him.*'

She sighed. 'If only Albert had remembered that earlier. Father and Henry have been gone for three years. That was probably his last letter, and it got thrown in the fire.' I waited for the tears, but Katherine's mouth was a hard firm line.

'But you said he hardly wrote when he was on one of his expeditions,' I said. 'No-one could have known. It was a chance remark. It's not surprising Albert forgot about it.'

Her mouth relaxed, and curled a little at the corner. 'I wish you would make your mind up.'

The fire was beginning to falter. 'I wish I could. I just don't know how I feel. One minute we're friends, and the next we're not.'

'Mm,' said Katherine. 'Friends.'

'Oh, stop it,' I said. 'You're as bad as my mother. He's probably only polite to me because I'm your friend and you're his cousin.'

'That's probably it,' said Katherine, a gleam in her eye. 'That's why he tells me off for getting you into scrapes, and does whatever you tell him, and gazes at you when he thinks no-one's looking. Because I'm his cousin.'

I was tempted to mention Mr King at this point, but dismissed the idea as being in rather poor taste. 'It doesn't matter, anyway. Albert clearly doesn't approve of the bicycles, and the sight of me riding one will probably put an end to it. Especially if I fall off.'

'I've just realised,' said Katherine. 'I could ride to the Department, and save the omnibus fare. That's how I'll get Aunt Alice on side. And I'll need to, or you'll never get a divided skirt.'

'That's an excellent point,' I said. I regarded Katherine speculatively. While she had assured me that her family could manage, it didn't take a great intellect to see the constant scrimping and saving. 'I would pay her for the time, of course. Would she alter more dresses for me as well, do you think?'

I could almost see Katherine's brain adding the balance. 'I imagine she might, although I still doubt she'll let you pay,' she said, noncommittally. 'I'll ask when she gets back.' She shot a sharp look at me. 'Will your mother mind you spending more money on dresses?'

I shrugged. 'If she's going to throw me at Albert she'll want me to be well-dressed.'

Katherine winced. 'Is she really doing that?'

126

'Yes.' I took another sandwich. 'Although when she saw the card from the Major she wasn't sure which way to jump.'

'And how do you feel?' Katherine put a hand on my arm.

I chewed as I considered the situation. 'I'd like to be able to make my own decisions without people pushing me all ways at once. And besides, I need to throw myself at another man.'

Katherine stared at me. 'I beg your pardon?'

I smiled. 'I need to find the man who was talking to me about tulips when Albert barged in at the Frobishers'.' I brushed my hands together to remove the crumbs. 'I need to find Toby Langlands.'

CHAPTER 17
Katherine

Miss Robson turned out to be an unexpected ally. Perhaps I shouldn't have been surprised. Although she and Aunt Alice had been friends from the time they were schoolfellows, they couldn't have been more different. Ever since she'd arrived as our lodger, Miss Robson had encouraged Aunt Alice to remember the fun they'd had as girls before they had had to become proper. She had watched the arrival of the bicycles from the window of her room, and managed to describe it to Aunt Alice in such a way that both of them were crying with laughter by the time she'd finished.

Miss Robson was very much in favour of my learning to ride, and asked if she might borrow Connie's bicycle on occasion until she obtained one of her own. Then, she said, perhaps we could join the ladies' wing of the local cycling club, which was, she was careful to point out, run by gentlemen and extremely respectable.

With some reluctance, Aunt Alice withdrew her objection, provided I wore proper clothes and didn't demean myself or the family with any form of divided skirt or knickerbocker. She refused to be moved on this point and as she was a far better seamstress than I, there was little I could do. By getting up earlier than normal every day to practice, Miss Robson and I, to the amusement of the neighbours' servants, learnt to ride in the narrow alley beyond the back of the house. Ada was not as amused. She was the one who would have to get the mud out of our skirts and petticoats.

On Thursday morning, I cycled to work for the first time. It meant enduring jeering men and jostling horses as best I could, but was preferable to the increasing sense that my footsteps were being dogged on my journey every day. Being a little early, I found one of our messenger boys and promised him a half-penny whenever I brought my bicycle in, if he could keep an eye on it for me. It was a price worth paying.

I had seen Reg being shown the ropes on Monday, and he had tipped his head a little in my direction, as if he wasn't entirely sure he was nodding at the right woman. But then he'd only seen me once, in a dimly lit room, under very different circumstances.

I didn't see Reg again until Thursday. He appeared in the typing room shortly before the morning tea-break, more or less pushed through the padded door by another lad, and stood slack-jawed. I sympathised.

I remembered my first day. I had been engaged after a short interview and a test of my capacity to manage one of the machines. The prerequisite seemed to be small fingers and a good level of education. I had never been anywhere like the typing room.

It was large enough for twenty desks in five rows, the supervisor's desk, and various cabinets and drawers for index cards. The ceiling was high, the walls tiled in green one third of the way from the floor and painted in another green above. Once a day, a boy armed with disinfectant spray would make a half-hearted sweep with a cloth on the tiles. A fireplace stood empty as if daring anyone to light it.

Motes of dust danced in undisciplined abandon in shafts of light from the tall windows, before falling onto neat piles of papers, stacked on the desks of straight-backed women in white blouses and dark skirts. They turned sheets of handwriting into typed reports without looking at their fingers.

The door sealed on baize, the windows had thin blinds, as if to hide the indecency of a room full of women from the world's gaze, rather than the other way about.

My ears had filled with rattle and clatter; a steady rhythmic *tap tap*, punctuated by periodic metallic sliding and crashing. I had closed my eyes and imagined myself in a chilly forge. A sucking of air and a soft thump had made me open my eyes. A boy, come to collect the typescript from the supervisor's desk. He had been thin, awkward, his ankles and wrists poking from his uniform, a red weal on the back of his neck where his collar dug in. Once he reached sixteen, he would no longer be allowed to enter.

Now I saw Reg as overwhelmed as I had been by the rattling keys, the rows of concentrating women, the swish of Miss Charles's skirt. He started as, with a squeak, the hatch in the wall opened and a tea-tray was proffered. In the same second, all the typing stopped and for a moment, there was silence but for small exhalations as we stretched and rolled our shoulders. Then the chatter began.

Pulling himself together, Reg walked down the aisle of desks as if checking our work. I was secretly proud of mine, since I often improved the English in the men's reports and letters. So far, no-one had noticed. Miss Charles turned to collect the tea-tray and, one by one, the women rose and arched their backs. I had just stood up when Reg came too close to my desk and knocked my papers off.

'Sorry Miss,' he said, bending to gather them up. I bent to help. After all, he'd have no idea what order they should be in. I gave him an encouraging smile; he must be nervous. I still wasn't sure if he recognised me. Reg's eyes met mine and he grinned. As he passed over the papers, I felt him slip a scrap of paper into my hand.

'Thank you Miss,' he said, very low. 'Ma wonders if you'd visit. She'd like to say thanks 'erself. This job could be the making of me.'

He stood and walked to Miss Charles as if to ask for instructions.

I tidied my papers and unfolded the note. It gave an address, written in neat, careful writing, in a street nearby and a request for me to visit, adding that I must not be afraid as Reg would accompany me. If I would like to bring my friend, she would be welcome too. It was signed Maria Edwards. I scribbled on the reverse of the note and handed it to Reg with my finished assignment before he withdrew.

The following evening, I wheeled my bicycle with Reg on one side and Connie on the other. We found ourselves in a street of small terraced houses, neat but tiny. Four families lived in the one Reg stopped at. Maria's had the

131

back room on the top floor. I regretted bringing Connie. If I felt rich in comparison, how must she feel?

'I'm sorry,' I whispered.

'Don't be,' she said.

I have no idea how the family managed in that tiny room. Maria and the little girl shared a narrow bed, and Reg must have slept on the extra mattress stored beneath. Maria sat at the small table with a workbox, teaching her daughter to thread needles and make neat stitches. Her mouth was narrow with effort.

'We're learning together,' she said, wiggling the fingers of her left hand. 'I'm learning to do it left-handed and she's learning right-handed. Maybe we'll be able to take on some work one day and help Reg out. But I'm so glad we managed to get him to school so he could learn to read and write. I'm so proud of him Miss, getting that job, and I'm so grateful to you for telling Mr King the job was going.'

I didn't know what to say. It seemed such a tiny thing, such a drop in the ocean of their desperation.

'Now let me pour you some tea,' said Maria, rising. 'I'm afraid I have no milk, but I do believe I have sugar.'

'No sugar for me, thank you,' said Connie and trod on my foot.

'Nor me, thank you,' I said.

Maria brought the tea, and we sat on the edge of the bed wondering what to say.

'It wasn't just to say thank you that I asked Reg to invite you here, Miss,' she said.

I sipped on the hot tea-flavoured water, my skin prickling.

'It was funny you saying about tulips,' she went on. 'I was a bit startled by Mr King bringing you in like that, and it meant nothing at the time. But then I remembered the letter.'

Connie and I exchanged glances. 'Do you mean the letter telling you that your old mistress had died?'

'No, not that one, the one what Reg got given.'

'I'm sorry, I...'

'It's like this,' said Maria, 'I left my mistress to get married, a year or so before Reg was born. She begged me to keep in touch which was a surprise. I think she was going a bit strange. I'd trained up a replacement good and proper, I was sure she'd be fine. I sent her a postcard now and then. Sometimes she'd send me one.'

Connie fidgeted and I felt the springs on the bed digging into me even through my petticoats.

'After a few years they stopped but by then I was busy with Reg and . . . the others. I had three more, Miss, what died, but that's the way things go, isn't it? And then I had little Martha and then a bit after, my husband died but I got a job in a factory and we were doing all right until the accident.' She lifted her right shoulder and her arm moved but her fingers remained flexed and paralysed. 'I worked on the sewing machines, Miss. Good I was. Of course it was hard with a little one, but we got by and then a machine came unbolted and fell on me when I was bending to pick up scraps.'

'That's terrible,' said Connie. 'Couldn't the doctor help at all?'

'No money for a doctor, Miss. Especially being out of work. They couldn't keep me on being useless like I am.'

'But . . . didn't the factory owner pay? It was his fault surely.'

Maria snorted. 'Not he. Still it's water under the bridge.

No point in crying over things you can't change, is it Miss? But I was a bit desperate so I wrote to my old mistress and got the reply from Gart to say she'd died. But that's not what I wanted to tell you.'

Reg was bouncing from foot to foot, 'Let me tell 'em Ma. You're taking too long. Thing is Miss Demeray, the other week, a bit before you turned up in our place I went out looking for work. Tramped all over I did. Got to bits of London I'd never seen with 'ouses so grand they touched the clouds. Ma said those sorts of places usually have a place for a strong lad. Coulda got an 'undred people inside and they'd have never bumped into each other if they didn't want to.'

Connie shifted beside me.

'I thought maybe I could get a job as a boot-boy or garden lad so I tried every one. But they just looked at me like I was dirt. One of the 'ouses was set back and shut up, and I saw apple trees behind. It was gettin' foggy, and I was thirsty, and 'ungry, and fed up.'

Reg paused for a moment. 'I know it was wrong Miss, but I goes down the little path into the garden. No sign of nobody; I called out, honest I did. The downstairs shutters was all closed and most of the upstairs ones but not all. Anyway, like I said, I was 'ungry. And course, there was no apples on the trees and none in the shed, but lots rotting on the ground.

I took my jacket off and got a basket from the shed, then I picked up apples like it was my job in case someone did see me. After a bit I sat on the little wall by the kitchen where I'd left my jacket. I'd have ate a couple of apples but when I bit into one it was rotten. So I picked some nuts for Martha, shoved 'em in my jacket pocket, and made for 'ome.

When I got there, I found a letter in my other pocket."Lazy bugger," I thought, pardon my language, someone wants me to be postman for them. It was addressed to R Demeray in a street I never 'eard of. No stamp or nuffink. So I asks Ma what to do.'

'And I said someone must have dropped it, and someone else must have thought it was yours and shoved it in your pocket in one of the busy places. I said, you'd best post it and be a good neighbour. Reg looked that tired, I couldn't face making him tramp out to your street. I had a stamp put by and I thought, it doesn't hurt to be kind does it?'

Connie and I exchanged glances.

'Reg,' I said, 'do you think that letter might have been put in your jacket pocket while you were working in the garden?'

'Could've I s'pose.' Reg pondered. 'Yeah, the trees were down a path, and I 'ad my back to the 'ouse, mostly.'

'Did you recognise the writing at all?' Connie asked Maria.

'Hard to say, Miss,' said Maria. 'Writing's writing. All posh people write about the same, begging your pardon Miss. But anyway, now I recall, there was a tiny bit of scribble on the back.'

'But it weren't scribble,' said Reg. 'it was flowers, drawn in ink. I didn't remember till Mr King told us your name. And now you've asked the question, I don't reckon anyone put that letter in my pocket in Piccadilly or somewhere like it. I reckon they did it in that garden.'

Connie nudged me, and I looked at her. Her usually innocent blue eyes sparkled with mischief. 'Reg,' she said,

135

'could you find that house again?'

Reg sat up straight. 'Course I could, Miss.'

'Are you up for an adventure?' said Connie. 'I need to hire a detective.'

CHAPTER 18
Connie

We might have to wait to visit Reg's mysterious house, due to the demands of the Department, but at least I had my own line of enquiry to follow up in the meantime.

My first port of call was the library. I scanned the bookcases for a volume I had never consulted, but which Mother referred to both before and after any formal occasion. *Debrett's Peerage*. As I had expected, it was on a convenient shelf and showed signs of extensive usage. I took it down and sat on the library steps to peruse it.

'LANGLANDS', I read. 'Creation 1581, of Horsham, Sussex. Sir Peter Hamilton LANGLANDS, 12th Baronet, b. Dec 6th, 1835; 1. his father, Sir WILLIAM LANGLANDS, 1868; ed. at Shrewsbury and at Trin. Coll., Camb…'

I scanned down the page.

'Sons living —' Toby, or Tobias to give him the full version, was three lines down, fifth in a list of five. And there were sisters, too. That was probably why Maisie

Frobisher had described him as 'no-one to bother about'. He would be too far down the list of eligible bachelors to concern her. But where did they live? 'Residence, Lowndes Square, S.W.' From the look of it, there was no seat, no country house. That must be what Toby had meant about his grandfather spending the family fortune on a wild goose chase after black tulips. Poor Toby. I sighed and closed the book. At least I knew that he was in London, but the question now was how to approach him in a decorous manner.

I stood up to replace the book; but as I did, something slipped down in the book; a slip of paper, meant to mark a place. I opened the book to tuck it in more securely, and was confronted by a host of Fs. FAIRBAIRN, FAIRBANK, RAMSAY-FAIRFAX, FALKINER —

I gasped, not from surprise as much as horror. I should have expected it.

Mother had been checking up on the Major.

'What are you reading?'

I jumped, slammed the book shut, and glared at Jemima, who had sneaked in and was regarding me with a mixture of suspicion and disdain. 'Nothing.' I fumbled it back onto the shelf.

'It's a very nicely-bound nothing,' she remarked, smirking. No doubt she had recognised the book. 'Anyway, I was sent to find you. Lunch is ready, and Mother wants to know what you're wearing to go to the Carrolls.'

'I'm having my green silk altered,' I replied.

'Let out?' Jemima asked, her eyes settling on my bosom.

'Updated,' I said firmly. 'I don't have an extensive trousseau or coming-out clothes on order.'

'Poor Cinders,' said Jemima cheerfully. 'Never mind. Perhaps one day your handsome prince will come. In fact,' — her eyes sparkled — 'maybe he already has.'

'I don't think so,' I retorted.

'No,' she said thoughtfully. 'He'd need a very big slipper, wouldn't he?' And she was gone before I could think of a suitable reply.

I suspected I would not have as much freedom at the Carrolls as I had at the Frobishers. For one thing, Jemima would spoil any fun that was to be had. And I couldn't rely on Toby Langlands being there, since it was a smaller and therefore more exclusive dinner.

The problem occupied me during lunch, to the extent that Mother asked if I was feeling ill again. 'You've barely eaten a thing, Constance,' she remarked, then frowned. 'I hope I won't have to send apologies to the Carrolls for you. Important people will be there.'

I suspected she meant the Major. 'I am quite well, Mother,' I said hastily. 'I was just thinking about a new evening bag, to go with my green silk. I saw a lovely one in Oxford Street.'

My mother inclined her head with something like approval. 'I have the carriage this afternoon, so you'll have to get a cab.' And she returned to dissecting her sole.

The first thing I did was send a wire from the nearest telegraph office. *Will be at Monk's draper's in Oxford Street. Need help, C.* I had barely selected and paid for a bag when a cab drew up outside with a great deal of snorting and stamping, and Albert leapt out. He peered through the window and I waved, at which his eyebrows knitted.

'I thought you were in trouble,' he said, as soon as I left

the shop. 'I've rushed here to rescue you.'

'From the draper?'

He shrugged. 'You got drugged at a tea-shop, remember? I didn't even wait for Tredwell to get the carriage out.'

'I'm sorry, I didn't think.' I did feel rather guilty.

Albert smiled then, and offered me an arm. 'What sort of help do you need, Connie? I hope it wasn't to choose anything. I'm not very good at that sort of thing, I leave it to my tailor.'

'No, no,' I assured him. I could feel my face beginning to glow at the idea of Albert helping me to choose clothes, of any kind. 'It was to find someone. I thought you might know him, and I need to talk to him.'

Albert stopped dead and I felt his arm stiffen in mine. He stared down at me. 'You want me to find a man for you?'

'That isn't how I mean it,' I said, quickly.

'I should hope not,' he said. He had released my arm now, and was glaring at me. A spot of colour showed in each cheek, and his eyes flashed blue.

'It's about the tulips —'

'Oh, hang the tulips!' He strode to the waiting cab and flung open the door.

'Wait!' I cried, feeling particularly small and stupid, clutching a brown-paper parcel in the middle of Oxford Street.

He turned, slowly. 'What.' It wasn't a question. It was a last chance.

I could feel tears coming, and I blinked to chase them away. 'Please, may we talk?'

***

We dismissed the cab at Hyde Park, and strolled down the leafless avenues while I tried to explain. I don't think I got half of it out, and what I did say probably didn't make much sense, but Albert seemed to understand.

'I see it a lot, from the other side,' he said. 'Married ladies of my acquaintance often bring their giggly younger sisters over and ask me to fill a space on their dance card so that they won't be disappointed. Of course they always are, because I don't dance very well, but that isn't really the point of it, is it.'

I sighed. 'I didn't think of it that way.'

'No.' He squeezed my arm. 'Ladies generally don't.' We walked for a while in silence. 'So who was it you wished to speak to?'

'A man called Toby Langlands. I was talking to him in the orangery at the Frobishers' when you — came to dance with me.' I had been going to say interrupted, but I didn't want to break our truce, which I sensed was still a little unstable.

'Oh, him,' said Albert. 'Yes, all right. I'll get him to come to my club tomorrow for a game or two of billiards, and meet you here?'

'That would be perfect,' I said. 'How do you know him?'

'Oh,' he said vaguely. 'I was at Rugby with one of his brothers. Been to their place a few times.'

I sighed. If Katherine and I were as well-connected as Albert, we would probably have solved this case a fortnight ago.

***

'So that was why your father gave the painting to the National Gallery,' I said.

We were sitting on two benches in Hyde Park, conversing out of the side of our mouths. The men were lounging together, while I sat straight-backed and demure as I could manage. The last thing I needed was some busybody friend of Mother's noticing my deportment and reporting my activities to her.

'Yes,' said Toby. 'He couldn't stand the sight of it. My grandfather sold his horses, his carriages, the paintings, even the country pile in the end, and all for a dream of a black tulip. The painting you saw was the only one that he kept.'

'But why?'

Toby shrugged. 'Tulip fever.'

'And he didn't get anywhere with the search?'

'Nobody knows. He didn't talk about it to anyone. But I doubt it. My father doesn't talk of it often, but he once told me that towards the end, when almost everything was gone, grandfather was very ill. They found sheets and sheets of paper in the study, scrawled with random words and question marks. No-one could make sense of it. He died shortly afterwards.' He fidgeted with his cuffs. 'I'd rather you didn't speak of this.'

'I won't,' I hastened to assure him. 'Thank you.' Then I paused. 'Why did you mention it at the Frobishers'?'

He smiled, sadly. 'I'd had a bit too much port, and when I saw you sitting alone, I remembered you'd been sitting next to that shouty man at dinner. And you looked — approachable.'

'That's been very helpful, Langlands,' said Albert, brushing his trouser-knees down and getting up. 'I'll see this lady into a cab, and then we'll have that game of billiards. I wager five pounds that I can take a game off

142

you.'

'You'll let him win, won't you?' I said, as soon as we were out of earshot.

'Of course,' said Albert. 'Not by too much, though. A man does have his pride.'

CHAPTER 19
Katherine

On Saturday afternoon, Albert's carriage picked Reg and me up a few streets away from the office. He and Connie seemed companionable enough, but there was a sense of awkwardness about them both, as if someone had said something the other person had misinterpreted. I wanted to bang their heads together.

'Is this really necessary, K?' said Albert, hauling Reg, who was sticking his head out of the window, back onto his seat like a gentleman. 'Can't you just go through Uncle Roderick's papers?'

I groaned. 'Do you think I haven't tried? You really have no idea what they're like. You've seen his bookshelves. He thought it was bordering on sinful to organise books. "They like to mingle," he'd say. His paperwork is very much the same. Until he hired Henry as a sort of secretary, everything was bundled up any old how. I found a letter to my grandmother about his birth in

144

1830, an enquiry about phoenixes from 1857, a daguerreotype of who knows what, a receipt for a pair of worsted stockings, a visiting card from someone who must have been dead for sixty years, and a sketch map of who knows where, tied up with gardening twine and put in a leather bag.'

'Maybe they're clues.'

'No Albert, they're just disorganisation.'

'Do you think this is necessary?' he repeated. We were now in Grosvenor Crescent and I could see what Reg meant about the houses. They made even Albert's house look as if it needed to try harder.

We pulled up at the one Reg remembered, and stood on the pavement. For once, I was glad of my plain clothes. Albert and Connie looked like a smart couple who had brought two staff to ensure their afternoon went smoothly. The house had a discreet sign outside, indicating it was for sale to the discerning wealthy. That was a stroke of luck as it meant we might not appear too suspicious.

Every visible window was shuttered, although it was impossible to tell about the servants' attic windows behind the parapet. The house looked forgotten and sad. Leaves covered the grand steps, and cobwebs had formed in the corners of the tall lower window frames.

We passed through the gate and into the garden at the rear. It was little more than a kitchen garden of course, being a London house, and we looked up at the ugly back of the house with its plumbing and grimy windows. The apple trees, asleep, hunched in the cold air. A herb garden had gone to seed before it slept and straggled across the unswept paths. Peering in through the kitchen windows, I saw a thin layer of dust.

Reg rubbed his hands.

'Easy as pie,' he said. He pointed at a small window in what was presumably a scullery. It didn't quite fit, as if it was more used to being open than closed.

'It looks awfully small,' objected Albert.

'Yeah,' said Reg, 'but so am I. It's good to be a short-house sometimes, ain't it Miss?' He winked at me and I couldn't help but grin back.

Reg slipped into the garden shed and came out dressed in his own clothes, leaving his office uniform with me. Then he opened the scullery window with worrying dexterity, dropped his satchel in and wiggled after it.

Waiting for him to return seemed to take a year. We walked round the garden and pointlessly peered into windows which were shuttered, and pretended to pace out the dimensions. Evening approached, and the garden grew darker. The street lamps would soon light up. Albert had told his driver to return in an hour, but the hour dragged. We were all tense, wondering if someone had reported us and whether, before we knew it, a policeman would appear and ask awkward questions to which we had no sensible answers. The house felt empty. I can't explain how you know, but I did know. There was no-one but Reg inside. The garden, however, seemed to be watching us.

My skin prickled, as it had most days on my journey to and from work for over a week. I was torn between staying close to Albert and Connie, hunting in the dark corners of the garden with a stick, or running away.

'I hope Reg is all right,' said Connie. Albert moved closer and put his arm round her shoulder for as long as it took him to remember this was improper. He let go of her as if she was on fire, then they separated as if nothing had happened and wandered in opposite directions. Once again, I wished I was tall enough to bang their heads together.

Unable to bear any of it much longer, I went round the side of the house, seeing if I could find any clues whatsoever on those rough Tudor bricks. A soft whistle made me jump. I looked up and saw Reg at another small window. He dropped his satchel into my arms and then slipped out himself, landing silent as a cat.

'Someone's talking to Miss Swift out back, so I come out this way,' he said. 'Cor. Fancy or what? I done drawings of what I seen, Miss. It's sort of an 'obby. Ma encouraged me cos she said it might lead to something one day — used to joke I could be an architeck or draw pictures for the papers. I've only got a couple of pencils and scraps of paper bags, though.' In the dimming light, he looked a little embarrassed.

'That's a really useful hobby for a detective,' I said.

He brightened and continued. 'There's loadsa stuff, but most of it's covered in sheets. And I took some rubbings too. I could tell there was carvings on things but I couldn't see 'em. It feels all empty, Miss. Sad. Some of the rooms felt — sadder than the others.'

Footsteps approached and we pressed ourselves against the ivy, but it was Albert and Connie, coming out from the garden arm in arm and grim-faced, as if they owned the place but didn't care for it. They relaxed as soon as they saw us.

'Come on,' whispered Connie. 'We need to go. The gardener popped up and started asking questions. Albert made something up on the spot which made less sense than if we'd told him we were burglars.'

'I'm not a natural dissembler, Connie,' said Albert. 'But

147

here's the carriage, not a moment too soon.'

In the carriage I sat back and breathed for what felt like the first time in an hour.

'Time to get you home, young man,' said Connie. 'You've earned at least a shilling.'

'What, me?' said Albert. She gave him a playful push. I rolled my eyes.

'So what did the gardener say?' I asked.

'He said that the owner had died some time ago and the place was up for sale, but the furniture would be auctioned,' said Connie.

'Perhaps we should get an order to view from the estate agents.' I said.

'That would have been the most sensible thing to do in the first place,' said Albert.

'Mmm,' said Reg. He was munching on a handful of raisins he'd presumably 'borrowed' from the kitchen. 'Thing is,' he said, 'I've been all round London these last few weeks and I ain't never seen that estate agent's name before.'

The sense of unease returned.

'Connie,' I said, 'what did the gardener look like?'

'Tall, thin, gaunt,' she said, 'He had a really strange way of moving, as if his back was more articulated than normal. And he stared as if he wanted to mesmerise us.' She shuddered.

She was describing the man from the omnibus. 'Jack Spratt'.

The Viper.

CHAPTER 20
Connie

'Stop the carriage!' Katherine shouted, and we jolted to a halt, causing a barrage of yells as other vehicles were forced to pull up sharply.

Albert peered out of the back window. 'On to the next side-street, please, Tredwell.' The hullabaloo ceased as we moved off. 'What's up, K?'

'It was him,' said Katherine, in a low voice, as if she might be overheard even in a closed carriage. 'That gardener was the Viper.'

'The Viper?' said Reg. 'Sounds like 'e came out of a penny dreadful.'

'Yes,' said Katherine. 'It does. But that's what Miss Holland called him. I saw him at Hendon, with a bright-eyed woman. The Magpie. They're the people who are keeping Miss Holland prisoner.'

I felt a cold hand around my heart, squeezing. Like a coiling snake. 'And we spoke to him, in the garden.' Albert's hand, warm through his glove, held mine tightly.

149

'It means we're on the right track.' Katherine rubbed her face with her palms. 'We should go back and do a proper search.'

'No,' said Albert, firmly. 'We should get help. I'm going to wire King. And I'm also going to fetch my pistol. If we're dealing with criminals, we need to be well-armed.'

We stopped at the next telegraph office, and Albert jumped out. 'Won't be long,' he said.

We waited, starting at every little noise. Katherine's eyes fell on Reg's satchel. 'Can we see the drawings, Reg?' she asked. 'The street-lamp will give us enough light.'

He grinned, and opened his satchel. 'Thought you'd never ask. Some of 'em *I've* barely seen.'

Katherine leafed quickly through the sheets of paper. There were sketches of grand fireplaces, sheeted furniture dwarfed by the grand proportions of the room it slept in, and even an occasional chandelier. Then she came to the rubbings, and exclaimed. 'Look!'

I peered at the sheet. There, blurred but discernible, was the outline of a stylised tulip. 'Where did this come from, Reg?'

Reg frowned. 'It was downstairs, on a frame. Couldn't see the picture, but the frame felt strange.'

'I'm sure it did,' said Katherine, grimly.

I shrieked as Albert stuck his head through the carriage window. 'I've wired him at the paper and his house, saying to meet us outside the place at nine. Hopefully one of 'em will reach him.' He opened the door and sat down beside me. 'I didn't mean to startle you,' he said, looking contrite.

'I didn't mean to shriek,' I said. 'It was just — I'm a bit nervous.'

Katherine leaned forward and patted my hand. 'We all are.'

'I think I ought to take you two home,' said Albert.

'No,' said Katherine. 'I was the person she wrote to. I have to go back. I feel — responsible, somehow.'

'And if she goes, I go,' I said, though I could hear the wobble in my voice.

'But what about your mother?' asked Katherine. 'I don't want you to get into trouble.'

I shrugged. 'I'm probably in trouble already,' I said. 'I generally am, and at least I'll know why this time.' I considered the situation. 'What I will do is send a wire that I'll be back late, and not to worry.'

'That's a good idea,' said Katherine. 'I'll do the same.'

'And then what?' said Albert.

'Let's do something to take our minds off it,' said Katherine.

***

We ended up at a song-and-supper room in Drury Lane, eating oysters and drinking champagne. Reg was having the time of his life, despite only being allowed beer. 'Keep a clear head for later,' Katherine warned. 'You might need it. We can't have you stumbling about all over the place, can we?'

'No, miss,' said Reg, shiny-faced and beaming.

I made a poor supper, and the oysters and champagne didn't sit particularly well together. 'Are you worried?' asked Albert, quietly.

I thought it over. 'A bit,' I said. 'But I'm excited too. Imagine if we find Miss Holland tonight, and rescue her, and solve the riddle of the black tulips.'

'Yes.' Albert's face was uncommonly serious. He

151

caught my look, and smiled. 'Let's hope we do.'

***

We returned to the house at nine, leaving the carriage fifty yards down the street. There was no sign of Mr King. 'What if he doesn't come?' I asked, feeling scared again.

'Then we'll manage,' said Katherine firmly.

We waited until five minutes past the hour, then ten. 'I can't stand much more of this,' said Albert. 'Come on.' He patted the gun in his coat pocket, and led the way round to the back of the house. As before, the garden gate was unlocked, and no lights showed at the windows. 'Reg, it's time to do your stuff. See if you can get a door open.'

'Right you are, sir,' said Reg. He crept forward, and was soon lost in darkness. Two minutes later I heard a creak, and a faint whistle. We advanced, cautiously. 'Come on,' Reg whispered, hoarsely. 'Scullery door's open. They left the key in.'

I sighed with relief. That meant we hadn't aroused their suspicions earlier. I stepped over the threshold. 'Do you think we should put the lights on?' I muttered.

'Not till we're sure that gardener's gone,' said Katherine. 'We could find a candle, though, they're bound to have some.'

A match flared, and I saw Albert's face in the glow. 'There,' he said, pointing to a shelf. He crossed the room and put his hand in the box, lighting the candle with the last gasp of his match. 'Now then.' He went into the kitchen and moved a chair, scraping it across the tiles.

'What did you do that for?' hissed Katherine.

'To see if we hear anyone moving,' Albert replied. 'If not, we're probably safe to proceed.' How could he be so calm in these circumstances? This was a side to him that I had never seen.

We stood, and listened. The house was utterly silent. 'There you go,' said Albert. 'Probably best to stick to candles, though, just in case. If someone sees lights on in an empty house, they might come and investigate.'

We lit a candle each, and moved on. 'Is it worth looking in the downstairs rooms?' Katherine asked.

'Nah,' said Reg. 'They was all empty before.'

'We'll head upstairs, then,' said Albert. 'Give each other room, though. No sense in setting light to ourselves.'

The stairs barely creaked as we ascended. 'Which room did you find the tulips in, Reg?' I asked.

'Never mind that now,' said Katherine. 'Let's look for Miss Holland. Everything else can come later.'

'The bedrooms was empty too, though, miss,' said Reg. 'I tried all of 'em. She must've been took.'

'The attics then,' said Katherine, walking quickly down the corridor towards the servants' door. 'Come along.'

The stairs to the attic creaked monstrously, and I gave fervent thanks that the house was empty. Reg was right. Miss Holland had been spirited away, and once we'd checked these rooms, we could go. We moved quickly from room to room, peering between tea chests, pieces of old furniture, and rolled-up rugs.

Two doors remained, one with a key in the lock. Nothing in the first room but lumber. Katherine turned the key, and —

We gasped. There, lying on a mattress, was a woman in a nightdress, her grey hair hiding her face.

Katherine ran to her and knelt by her side. 'Wake up!' she whispered, touching the woman's shoulder.

At last, she stirred. Her eyelids fluttered open, and she

153

smiled. 'Good day,' she whispered. 'Have you come about the tulips?' She looked from one to another of us, her eyes roaming over us as if she were seeking someone in particular. Her smile broadened. 'I love spring flowers, but their season is so short.'

Katherine leaned closer to her. 'Her breath smells odd,' she said. 'Like alcohol, and spice.'

'That's probably the drug,' I said. 'She sounds as if she's under the influence.'

'What is your name?' asked Katherine, looking into the wrinkled face. 'Please tell us.'

'I am Mr Duncan.'

We whipped round, and my heart sank. Standing in the doorway was the man I had spoken to earlier. He held an oil lamp, and in the light his eyes gleamed.

'Don't try to barge me, now,' he said, closing the door and leaning his long back on it. 'My missus has gone for a policeman, and you'll be in more bother if you're taken up for assault.' And he smiled a slow, reptilian smile.

***

In some ways it was a good thing that the policeman was the one who had interviewed us at the tea-shop. 'You two again,' he grumbled. 'Caster and Fleet. The fainting ladies.' His mouth twitched. 'And what were you trying to do this time?'

'Find this lady,' said Katherine, indicating the form on the mattress, who was beaming as if we were putting on a performance especially for her benefit. 'She wrote the letters which were stolen at the tea-shop. We think she is being held against her will. And when we came to enquire earlier, Mr Duncan there told us that she had died.'

'Did he now?' The policeman turned to glare at Mr

Duncan, who stood flanked by his wife, standing with her bright eyes cast down. 'What do you have to say to that, sir? Why is this lady in the attic?'

Mr Duncan — the Viper — sighed. 'It's a long story, Constable. But the short version is that she is quite mad. It started some years ago, when she heard a story about a lost fortune in the family. Something to do with black tulips.'

My jaw dropped. I stole a glance at the others. Everyone's attention was fixed on Mr Duncan. Katherine opened her mouth to speak, then closed it.

'The lady became obsessed, writing letters, making trips, offering rewards for anyone who could give her information about black tulips. She followed leads which all came to nothing. She wouldn't stop, however much me and my wife pleaded with her. She shut herself away from the few friends she had left, devoting herself to a wild goose chase.' He shook his head sadly. 'Her physician advised that we should have her committed to an asylum, but we didn't have the heart. Imagine our mistress, chained up in a cell.'

'That isn't so different from the arrangement you have here,' Albert observed.

Mrs Duncan raised her head and glared at him. 'This isn't where my mistress normally sleeps,' she said, in a soft voice. 'It's only for when she is so deluded that she might do herself harm. There's nothing in here to hurt her, you see.'

'That's why we generally tell visitors that she's passed away,' Mr Duncan added, sadly. 'The truth is too painful.'

'Well,' said the policeman. 'It sounds like a misunderstanding on both sides.' He turned to Mr Duncan. 'Do you wish to press charges, sir?'

Mr Duncan looked at us all, considering. 'No,' he said. 'That wouldn't help anyone. All I ask is that you don't come back ever again. You know the truth now, and it isn't good for her to be disturbed.'

'That seems more than fair,' said the policeman. 'And it makes my job a lot easier, too.' He nodded to Mr Duncan, then turned to us. 'Now you lot, I want a word with you downstairs.'

***

Albert sent us to wait in the carriage while he spoke to the policeman. Eventually he returned, a rueful expression on his face. 'Drive on,' he said to Tredwell.

'Are you all right, Albert?' asked Katherine.

He held up two sheets of ruled paper. 'I offered to make a donation to the Metropolitan Police Orphanage in exchange for these. He was more than willing, but this paper didn't come cheap.'

'I'm sorry, Albert,' I said, biting my lip.

'Don't be,' he said. 'It was like being in a melodrama. And you found your letter-writer.'

'Who's mad,' I said, flatly.

'I'm not so sure,' said Katherine. 'I need to think about it.'

'I'll have plenty of time to think,' I snapped. 'Mother probably won't let me out of my room until the turn of the century.'

'We'll think of something,' soothed Albert. 'And at least we weren't grilled for too long. It's only a quarter past ten.'

'After ten!' I groaned. 'She'll kill me.'

I stared moodily out of the window. The streets still bustled with light and noise — people leaving restaurants,

156

couples walking, whispering and laughing, and paperboys shouting the evening edition like parrots.

'*Standard! Standard!* Latest news! Information wanted on a vicious assault!'

'Evenin' *Times*, Army officer at death's door!'

'Stop!' Everyone looked at me. I reached for the carriage door.

It felt like a bad dream as I walked towards the newspaper seller and exchanged a penny for a paper. I didn't need to open it. It was on the front page.

ARMY MAJOR ATTACKED IN BROAD DAYLIGHT
Assailants flee the scene
Victim in a critical state
Attack apparently unprovoked

Police are seeking information from anyone who witnessed an attack on Major Charles Fairbank in the Marylebone area yesterday. Major Fairbank, 52, served for many years in Africa...

I couldn't read any more. The newsprint blurred before my eyes. I walked to the carriage, got in, and put the newspaper into Albert's hand.

'What is it, Connie?' he asked, reaching out for me.

'They got him,' I said, through my tears. 'They got the Major.'

I felt the carriage move, I felt Albert's arms around me, but everything else was a haze of misery and guilt.

What had we done?

Chapter 21
Katherine

We took Reg home first and sent him in, with two shillings for himself, sixpence for Maria, and a note of apology.

'We're really sorry,' said Connie.

'You gotta be kidding!' said Reg. 'When can we do it again?'

Even though it was nearly eleven, he was undaunted, whistling as he went inside.

They dropped me off next and I scurried up the steps before the neighbour's bedroom curtains could flutter. The carriage rattled into the night. I braced myself, put my key in the lock and turned it as quietly as I could.

It was no good. Ada was dozing behind it. I tripped over her in the darkness, we both squealed, and I knocked a brass bowl off the hall table.

For a moment all I could hear was the slowing swirl of the spinning bowl on the tiles and my thudding heart. Then there was a rattle of door-handles and soft candlelight at the top of the stairs.

Aunt Alice ran down the stairs so fast the candle was about to blow out. Even in the flickering apricot glow, I could see tears in her eyes. She flung her arms round me and held me tight. 'You're safe, you're safe. Are you safe?'

'I'm so sorry.'

'You will be if you've dented that bowl,' said Ada. 'Here Madam, let me take that candle before you set fire to Miss Katherine's hat.' Oh dear. No 'Miss Kitty' tonight.

'I couldn't make head nor tail of your wire. I had no idea what had happened to you,' said Aunt Alice. 'What was Albert thinking? I trusted him to keep you safe.'

'I'm so sorry,' I repeated. She loosened her grip a little, looked into my face, and took a breath.

'Now go to bed and we will discuss this in the morning. But rest assured Katherine, I shall not let you out of my sight tomorrow. I promised your mother I'd look after you, and see how I've failed.'

'I'm sorry,' I said again as we mounted the stairs. I could just make out Margaret peeking from her room.

'You are in so much trouble.' I could hear the smirk. Inside my room, I undressed in darkness and climbed into bed. Ada, despite everything, had put a water bottle in for me. I hugged it, curled beneath the covers, but the chill would not go away.

What had we done?

***

In church the next morning I was placed at the wall end of our pew, as if Aunt Alice feared I might otherwise escape up the aisle. I was under strict instructions to listen properly so that I could repeat the main themes of the sermon, but my mind tumbled like flood water over

159

everything that had happened, and the vicar's words ebbed and flowed.

'Ask, and it shall be given you; seek, and ye shall find; knock, and it shall be opened unto you: For every one that asketh receiveth; and he that seeketh, findeth; and to him that knocketh it shall be opened... For where your treasure is, there will your heart be also.'

I stood, I sat, I knelt, I made my responses. I traced the shapes cut into the wooden pew and thought of picture frames. I peered up at the stained glass above me. The placid saint dropped her blue lilies and they fell as black tulips into my lap. Margaret nudged me awake.

After lunch we sat in polite silence as I picked at my meal, pushing my plate back half full. Listening, listening.

At two o'clock Hodgkins arrived with a note. He put it into my hand, tipped his hat, whispered something I couldn't make out and shrugged, before walking off.

The note was a folded piece of paper with two seals. *Dear Miss Demeray, I am writing to sever acquaintance with you. I must consider my reputation, and suggest you do the same. An excess of imagination has swept us away like a Fleet of ships on Caster oil. We must separate to Cultivate a sober life and Look in Higher places. Yours Constance Swift.*

How much worse could things get? Swallowing the lump in my throat, I folded it and went to throw it in the fire but Ada darted forward and snatched it out of my hand.

'Never destroy letters in haste,' she said. 'Your father never did. Says things sometimes need to brew. Besides, it's from your friend. I recognise the seal.'

'She's not my friend any more.'

'That's as maybe. I'll put it out of reach and give it

160

back later. You'll be glad.'

At four p.m. the door-bell rang. My heart thumped and I began to rise, but Aunt Alice startled me with a sharp 'Sit. Ada will answer.'

Moments later, Ada admitted Mr King.

'A Mr King to see you, Madam,' she said. 'Mr Bertie's friend with the bicycle.' She muttered 'Gallivanter'.

'Katherine,' said Aunt Alice, 'close your mouth. Ada, bring tea. Mr King, if you are a friend of Albert's, presumably you were involved in last night's excursion. Have you come to apologise?'

'He was not there, Aunt Alice,' I said.

'Hmmph,' she said, then sat more firmly in her chair.

'It's a pleasure to meet you, Miss Perry. I am sorry I was not able to make your acquaintance earlier,' said Mr King. 'I am not sure what has worried you. However, all appears to be well, and I know Mr Lamont would never take less than good care of Katherine.'

How could he know? Where had he been? His presence at the house might have made all the difference. I glanced at Aunt Alice to see if she would give us some privacy, but she settled herself even more firmly. I felt my irritation rise and forced it into my embroidery. Stabbing a needle through the daisies, I drove it into my finger. I winced and sucked at my finger. Blood sprinkled the embroidered flowers.

'Really, Katherine,' said Aunt Alice. 'One would think you were six years old.'

There was a silence.

'Everyone seems rather out of sorts,' said Mr King.

'I'm not,' said Margaret.

'Perhaps this might entertain you,' Mr King continued.

161

He withdrew some squares of fine paper from an inner pocket and started to fold them. Even Aunt Alice leaned forward. A box, a bird, a frog were formed with a few folds and twists.

'They're delightful,' said Aunt Alice.

'A Japanese man taught me,' said Mr King. 'This is for you, Miss Margaret.' He touched the frog and it hopped forward. 'And these are for you, Miss Perry.' He handed her the other things. 'Now something for Miss Demeray. People for a story.'

First he made a sleeping woman. Did I look that tired? I scowled at him but he would not meet my eyes. Then he made a thin man and a short woman in a long full skirt. Margaret laughed. '"Jack Spratt could eat no fat, his wife could eat no lean."'

I leaned forward.

'Maybe one more person,' said Mr King. 'Someone the others fear.'

He selected a sheet of paper the colour of shadow and started to fold. The figure he held up was ambiguous. One half was trousered, the other skirted.

'A fourth person,' he said, 'or a third waking person to watch the sleeping person.'

'Sleeping,' I said.

'Yes.'

'Is it a man or a woman?' said Margaret.

'I don't know,' said Mr King, 'that has yet to be revealed. But we shall find out.' This time his eyes met mine.

***

The following morning Aunt Alice raided her little money box and paid for a cab to take me to work. It was

162

pointless arguing that it was ridiculous for a typist to turn up in a cab.

'And I expect you home by half past five. If not for me, in memory of your mother.'

I persuaded the cabbie to drop me off a few streets earlier and walked the remainder. I longed to be able to wire Connie. Ada had given me Connie's letter now that I had had a good night's sleep, and told me to read it again. I hadn't, unable to face seeing those heartless words, and hoped that for once they'd lit the fire in our room as the typing paper was curling in the cupboard from the damp.

I was disappointed. The room was as chilly as ever. In any event Miss Charles was on the warpath. One of the girls had sent a message to say she had a fever and would not be coming to work, but a governmental crisis was going on and our workload was overwhelming. I hadn't seen Reg and was starting to worry, but he appeared, nonchalant as ever, with the morning tea and handed me a note.

It was not Maria's writing this time and I presumed it was his own. It was quite baffling: *The lady's Ma's Missus. Tell you on the steps outside, lunch time. Tell Miss Swift. Reg.*

I put the note in my bag and pulled out Connie's. *Connie's.* What had she signed herself? I reread the note. Constance. She never called herself Constance. And two seals. Why two? One had her crest but the other was a blob of wax with scratches on it. I squinted and fetched the magnifying glass we had for particularly illegible handwriting. Scratched into the wax was a flower.

It was almost impossible to concentrate now; but I had to, or risk overtime. Somehow, my fingers flew, doubling

163

my typing speed and yet managing to meet Miss Charles's exacting standards.

At lunchtime I rushed out into the rain, and stood on the steps waiting for Reg.

A woman huddled in an old-fashioned raincoat was standing at the bottom, her back to me. The coat looked like Father's but that was ridiculous. Aunt Alice? No, too tall. The woman turned as if she knew I was watching, and her face was anxious.

'I'm so sorry,' said Connie. 'Mother made me write, I hoped you'd know it was false.'

'I…' I started.

''Ow do, ladies!' Reg bounced down the steps. ''Ave I got news for you!'

'I'm sorry we got you home so late, Reg,' said Connie. 'I hope your mother will forgive us.'

'Well, you know,' said Reg, rubbing his ear as if in memory of his welcome, 'I described the house and she said "That sounds like Grosvenor Crescent, where I worked when I was a maid. Dovecote House. My missus called me Mary, she did. She said Maria was too fancy." And you'll never guess what else.'

'Come on, let's get out of this rain so you can explain. We need lunch,' said Connie. 'I didn't have breakfast. I had to climb out of the window in the middle of the night and try and get to your house before you left for work. It didn't go to plan, as you can tell, but I'm here now and starving.'

I would have hugged her if she hadn't been so wet.

'Really, Connie,' I said, 'And your Mother thinks *I'm* the bad influence.'

Connie shrugged as we entered the restaurant where

we'd first met.

'Never mind me,' she said. 'Reg, can you find us a table while I hang up my things?' As he skipped away, she leaned closer, 'I don't know what he's going to tell us, but he's in danger and so is Maria. I've been reading about the Major. Those people are not playing games.'

CHAPTER 22
Connie

'Her name's Miss Gregory,' said Reg, between gulps of stew. 'Thirza Gregory.'

'Thirza Gregory,' I said, trying the name out. It all seemed much more serious now that we were dealing with a real person, with a life and servants and connections, and not the fictional 'Miss Holland'.

'Yus.' Reg chewed on a bit of gristle. 'And Ma was her maid till she left to marry. That was back in 1874.' His eyes widened, as if such a span of time was inconceivable. 'But Miss Gregory wrote her letters, though Ma said she couldn't make out much of it. Hints about a family secret, and searching for something, and not knowing what the tulips meant.'

'Does she still have the letters?' asked Katherine.

Reg shook his head. 'She kept 'em for years, she said, but when we couldn't afford kindling no more, they went on the fire.'

Katherine pinched the bridge of her nose. 'Who else

was in the household? Did she say?'

Reg grinned. 'Oh yus.' He scraped his plate with a piece of bread, and dispatched it with a great swallow. 'There weren't many, just Ma and the housekeeper an' the cook and butler-man. An when she described him, I swear it was the bloke what caught us the other night. She said the cook and butler were man and wife. Mr an' Mrs Duncan.'

'The Viper and the Magpie,' breathed Katherine, leaning forward. 'And what about the housekeeper? Did your mother say much about her?'

'She didn't like her much, when she was there. She called her the Skellington.' Reg grinned. 'No love lost between 'em, I reckon. Apparently she was a very good housekeeper, always knew when someone had had more than their share. Paring away at the meals, slicing the bread thin, stinting on the currants in the cakes. And Ma thought this housekeeper, Gart she was called, got worse once she left. Miss Gregory sounded scared of her. She wrote that Gart was trying to steal her secret from her, and the family fortune with it. Ma even thought about visiting to see what was up, but by then she couldn't afford it.'

'If only we'd known,' I said. 'We could have done something.' I tried another spoonful of the grey stew, which I had selected for reasons of economy, but it was no better than the first spoonful had been. I saw Reg eyeing it, and pushed the plate his way.

'We're doing something now,' said Katherine. 'Or trying to.' She sighed. 'It's so hard when the clues aren't there any more. Like trying to finish a jigsaw puzzle with half the pieces missing.'

'At least we have another piece or two now,' I said, as

brightly as I could. 'And perhaps there are more. Reg —'

Reg froze, spoon halfway to mouth.

'Did your mother say anything else about this Mrs Gart?'

'Miss,' Reg corrected. 'She said that while Gart was all starched white collar'n cuffs and that, she wouldn't have wanted to meet her in a dark alley. "There's somefink of the night about Miss Amy Gart," she said, and didn't Ma look grim when she said it.'

Katherine's shoulders stiffened. 'Miss Amy Gart,' she repeated. She fumbled in her bag, drawing out a crumpled envelope and a pencil, and printed the name, letters separate.

Reg leaned over and inspected it. 'Nearly, miss.' He took the pencil and scratched out the Y, replacing it with an I and E. 'Like that, A—M—I—E. Ma remembered because Gart said it meant friend, and she was the least friendly person Ma's ever known.'

Katherine stared at the paper, then picked up the pencil and wrote the letters again, in a circle. Then she wrote a word below, and pushed the envelope towards me.

ARMITAGE.

***

I almost felt envious of Katherine and Reg. They had an afternoon of work ahead of them; somewhere they could think of other things, and, of course, earn money. I had paid for their lunch, partly out of habit, and while I had put all the money I had in my purse, I knew it might have to last me a while. Particularly as I wasn't sure where I would be sleeping that night.

Mother had restrained herself while Albert apologised on my behalf, and told a story about a damaged wheel on the carriage. She even managed a thank you. However, the moment the carriage could be heard leaving, she rounded on me with such ferocity that I took a step back.

'Am I going to have to send you to the countryside?' she shouted.

I swallowed. 'I don't know what you mean, Mother.'

If anything, that made her angrier. 'Ha! You don't know enough to keep yourself out of trouble, Constance.' She lowered her voice. 'Do I have to send your father round to *his* father, to arrange matters?'

I gasped. 'No!' I cried.

'Let's hope not,' Mother said, a little more calmly. 'But I shall make this clear, Constance. You will not associate with that man, or his cousin Miss . . . Demeray any longer.' She sighed. 'I knew I should have been more careful. For all I know she only pretended to be your friend to lure you into that man's clutches.'

'That isn't true,' I said, drawing myself up.

'True or not,' she countered, 'your friendship is over. You will write a note to that effect in the morning. Go to bed and stay there.'

She stood over me the next day while I wrote the note to Katherine. I tried to drop a hint that it wasn't my will, but I cried as I wrote. I knew I would never have a chance to explain.

Mother read the letter. 'Good, if a little rambling,' she said. 'Once that is posted, it will be the end of the matter. No.' She held up a hand as I made to get up. 'You will stay in your room today. I have told Parker to make sure there is a servant on guard at all times. You can have meals on a tray.'

'When can I come out?' I asked, my heart sinking.

'When I am satisfied that you have learnt your lesson.'
Mother swished away, leaving Mary — Mary was already
stationed outside — to close the door behind her.

I wept for a while before realising that it did nothing but
made me feel more miserable. I would never learn my
lesson. Mother would not be happy or satisfied until I was
a graceful, smiling automaton, and that would never
happen.

And it was then that I realised what I had to do.

Father came to see me that afternoon. He had come in
from a walk, and the fresh-air smell in my stale room was
another reminder of my status as prisoner. 'Um, your
mother has asked me to have a word with you,' he said,
laying his overcoat on the armchair.

'Has she,' I said, dully.

'Yes. She, ah, didn't make the detail quite clear, but...'
He paused, as if taking a mental run-up at the next part.
'You should try and take her advice, and be a good girl.
There.' He put an awkward hand on my shoulder, and I
burst into sobs. After a couple of nervous pats, he fled.

Once I was sure he had gone, I jumped up and put his
coat at the back of my wardrobe. That would help
considerably.

I ate all my meals, like a good girl, and when Mary
came to say goodnight, I was already in bed. 'I'm very
tired,' I sighed. 'Being locked up is boring.'

'It'll seem better in the morning, Miss Connie,' she
said, smoothing my pillow, and I wondered what they were
saying in the servants' hall. 'Sleep in, and I'll bring your
tray at ten.'

'Thank you, Mary,' I said, settling back on my pillows
and closing my eyes.

It was still dark when I woke. I lit a candle, and the mantel clock said twenty past four. Perfect. I dressed in the warmest clothes I had, with Father's coat over the top, and filled my bag and pockets — pockets! — with things which might be useful; money, jewellery, a pencil and notebook, a small sewing kit, hairpins. I would have to travel light.

I raised the window sash gently, with barely a squeak, and peered out. This would be the worst, since my room was on the first floor. I did not want to add an unsuccessful escape and a broken ankle to my list of defects. But a drainage pipe passed my window, and with some shifting and wriggling, my bag between my teeth, I managed to grab it and slide most of the way down, landing feet first in a flowerbed. 'Sorry,' I whispered to the squashed blooms. The garden gate creaked a little, but it could have been the wind. I pulled Father's coat around me, turned the collar up, and walked on.

***

And now here I was, free as a bird and with time on my hands until Katherine and Reg finished for the day. I had already wired Albert that morning. *Not at home but safe. Burn this. C.* I wished I could see him, and pour out the horrible things Mother had said — and that was exactly why I couldn't see him.

I thought of visiting Mr King, at the newspaper, but . . . I was still cross with him. If he had come to help us, we might have been able to save Miss Gregory and come out triumphant. He hadn't given any explanation, or apology, beyond vague assurances to Katherine and a set of paper figures.

And anyway, I was still hungry. Reduced circumstances or not, I might as well enjoy a meal, but where?

171

I roamed the streets, collar turned up and hat pulled down, listening at every step for a cry of 'Miss! Stop there, Miss!' and a police whistle. For all I knew, Mother had set the whole Metropolitan Police Force on my trail. But I walked undisturbed, and my footsteps led me to the tea-shop where Katherine and I had drunk that ill-fated tea. I paused, then decided to trust to fate, and went in.

The same waitress hurried up, already wringing her hands. 'Oh madam, I'm so sorry about what happened, and so glad you've come back! Is the other lady all right?'

It was the most effusive welcome I had had for days. 'Oh yes, it was — a temporary indisposition.'

'Oh, that does put my mind at rest. I'll make sure to let the doctor know. He did come in asking after you a few days later. He said the policeman hadn't taken your address.'

'No,' I said. 'He didn't.' I picked up the menu. 'But I could visit his practice and let him know.'

'It's Dr Bradley, in Connaught Street. It's only round the corner,' the waitress said, encouragingly. 'Now what can I get you?'

'A beefsteak, boiled potatoes and vegetables,' I said firmly. 'And a glass of water.'

***

'I didn't think I'd see you again,' said Dr Bradley, sitting behind his desk. 'I assume you're not here for an examination.'

'No, indeed.' I smiled. 'I wondered if you could tell me what you found in the teapot.'

Dr Bradley opened the top drawer of his desk, rummaged among the papers, and drew out a sheet of paper, which he frowned at. 'Laudanum,' he said. 'But

172

you're the second person to come asking. A young man turned up about a week ago, saying he was enquiring on your behalf. Said he was your brother. He described the pair of you well enough.'

I thought for a moment. 'A dark-haired man, with a moustache?'

'Indeed he was,' said the doctor.

That description fitted Mr King. He seemed to be cropping up more and more. 'Did he enquire about anything else?' I asked.

Dr Bradley considered. 'Not that I recall. Should I not have said anything?'

'No, no, it's quite all right. But perhaps not in future.'

'Well, if that's all —'

'No!' I cried, and he paused, mid-rise. 'You could help us. With a second opinion.'

The doctor lowered himself into his chair. 'On whom?'

'A lady,' I said. 'She's being kept prisoner in her own home, and I think she's being drugged with laudanum. By the same people who gave it to Miss — Caster and me.'

The doctor's eyebrows couldn't climb any higher. 'You're sure about this?'

'Yes.' I swallowed. 'She wrote us letters, and we've been trying to find her. Her servants have been telling people that she's dead, and they told us she's mad. We found her in the attic of her own home, delirious, and her breath smelt — odd. My friend said it was like alcohol and spice.'

'I see.' The doctor steepled his fingers. 'Have you informed the police?'

I snorted. 'The servant called one, but it was the same constable you dealt with at the tea-shop. He chose to regard

173

it as a misunderstanding.' I sighed. 'He'll probably be watching out for us. That's if they haven't taken her away.'

'Mmm.' Dr Bradley picked up a pen, looked at it, and put it down. 'Something tells me that I had better not produce any written evidence about this,' he said, with a wintry smile. 'When did you find this lady?'

'On Saturday evening,' I said.

The doctor thought. 'I doubt they would move her that night, or the next day. That would look suspicious. If she is drugged, she would be hard to move in any case. And if they let her come round, and she is mad, her behaviour would be unpredictable.'

'And they would need to find somewhere secure to move her to,' I said.

'Quite.' The doctor smiled again. 'Well, Miss —'

'Swift,' I said. I felt it was only fair. 'But don't tell anyone.'

'I suspected as much,' he twinkled. 'There is more than enough to interest me here. However, I have a surgery full of patients awaiting my attention.'

My face fell.

'After five o'clock tonight, however, when my practice hours end, I am at your disposal.' His face grew serious. 'But if I find that this is a hoax —'

'Oh, no, doctor, I promise.'

He nodded. 'Your face shows your conviction. Very well. Come back at five o'clock, and we shall see.'

The first thing I did was wire Albert. *Meet me at 35 Connaught Street, 5 o'clock sharp. Going back in with doctor. DO NOT TELL MR KING. C*

I glanced at the clock on the telegraph-office wall. It was a quarter to three. How on earth could I fill the time?

And what about Katherine and Reg? They finished work at five, but they had to be there.

I counted the money in my purse, sighed and put it away before leaving. How much would it cost to buy their freedom for the rest of the day? Whatever the price, I told myself, it was worth it.

It had to be.

CHAPTER 23
Katherine

It seemed strange to think that when we'd first met, I'd thought of Connie as unconfident. The defiance she had shown her mother was worthy of Boadicea. She had not told me what had been implied about Albert, but I could guess. Poor Albert. The only man less likely to be a seducer was Henry. He had never attempted to kiss more than my cheek.

All the same, even Boadicea would have quailed in the emotionless face of the civil service. I toiled through the afternoon helping to clear the backlog, completely unaware that Connie was arguing with the doorman, with Miss Charles, and with the boys' superintendent, finding out for the first time that money can't buy everything when there are ministers to please.

At five minutes past five, I emerged to catch the cab Aunt Alice had ordered. Soon Connie and I would be able to discuss what we should do next.

'May I walk you home?'

I turned to find Mr King beside me. I wondered if he was distantly related to Ada, given the way he managed to appear from nowhere.

'My aunt insists I travel by cab till I learn to behave,' I said. 'Besides…' I indicated the weather.

'A bit of rain never hurt anyone,' said Mr King. 'Your aunt approves of me, I can tell. I just want to talk to you in private for a bit. I'll pay his fare and we'll walk. I have a large umbrella and am tall enough to use it without putting people's eyes out, unlike some I could mention.'

'Wotcher!' It was Reg, running to catch us up. 'What am I missing? I got sumfink for you Miss, wot the other lady left after she'd been rampaging.'

'Rampaging? Connie?'

'Yeah.' said Reg. 'You shoulda seen her in the foyer. She tried to get them to let both of us off this afternoon, arguing for England like a tiger, but they wouldn't let us go. Even soaked through she was fierce. If she'd been in that mood on Saturday, maybe we'd 'ave got somewhere.'

Mr King sighed, 'I'm sorry I was too late to help. I sneaked into the house in Grosvenor Crescent just before you were escorted off the premises. I eavesdropped until I stood on a loose floorboard. The man was alerted by the creak and I had to sneak back out. That policeman isn't so stupid that he wouldn't be suspicious if he found me there too. On Sunday, Miss Demeray, what I was trying to explain with the figures was…'

'That there's a third person involved in keeping Thirza Gregory captive.'

He frowned. 'How did you discover her name? I've spent the best part of the day trying to find it out.'

'She was Ma's missus,' said Reg. 'Wot she used to write to.' His smile had gone and his next words barely audible. 'Do you think she's in danger, Sir? Ma, I mean?'

Mr King was silent, then patted Reg's shoulder. 'She's a fighter, your Ma, isn't she? And we'll protect her, Reg, won't we? So right now, I want you to go straight home, quick as you can, and keep your family safe.'

Reg pulled his collar up as he contemplated the rain and prepared to dash into it. He rummaged in his pocket. 'All right, but 'ere's the note wot Miss Swift left with the superintendent. He just give it me now. Her writing's shocking.'

'It's not addressed to you,' I pointed out.

'Yeah, well,' said Reg, and ran off.

I ducked into a doorway and opened the note. The wind was driving the rain now and the paper flapped and dampened. I struggled to open it. Mr King read over my shoulder; 'Meet me at the house at half past 5. If we are not there, wait out of sight till we arrive. The doctor will help. DO NOT TELL MR KING. C.'

He blinked and rubbed his chin, and for a moment the usual smile in his eyes clouded. 'I'm hurt,' he said. 'I never thought there was a woman I couldn't win over.'

I was about to retort when I saw that although the words were jocular, his expression wasn't. He focused on me. 'Miss Demeray, which doctor does Miss Swift refer to?'

'I don't know,' I said. 'The only one I can think of is the one from the tea-shop.'

Mr King's face darkened further. 'I've changed my mind about the cab,' he said, stepping out into the road and raising his arm. 'That man was far too eager to let me know his analysis. I don't like him. You and Reg should go

178

home.'

'You really don't know me at all, Mr King,' I said. 'You're going nowhere without me.'

***

Mr King leant forward to peer out of the windows. I was not sure where we were, it was so hard to make out through the downpour.

The cab rattled and splashed through puddles. Rain water drove against the windows. In the dimming light we swerved and skidded.

'But the doctor was perfectly kind,' I argued. 'He believed there was something wrong with the tea, unlike that idiot of a policeman.'

'He was too smug,' said Mr King. 'Don't forget, you were under the influence of a powerful drug.'

'He seemed charming.'

'Mmm,' said Mr King, ' I can't explain it, but he was too charming. He should have been reluctant to tell me anything.'

'But he did.'

'Yes. He played reluctant but then I asked if I could donate to any charitable fund he might have. He happily took ten shillings and unaccountably he remembered everything, right down to your descriptions. I wanted to warn you. The reason I was delayed on Saturday evening was because I had an "urgent" wire from Dr Bradley asking me to go round to his practice. When I arrived, he asked if I'd found out any more about the mystery ladies with the drugged tea. I said no and left. But it worried me and more to the point, it delayed my arrival.'

Suddenly, Mr King jumped up and pulled down the window. 'Stop!' he shouted. Opening the door, he leapt out into the road. A carriage was racing towards us. Mr King waved his arms until, with the horses rearing above his head, the carriage stopped. I started to clamber out but he yelled at me, 'Get back inside!' We were blocking the traffic. Other vehicles were trying to get round us, cursing and splashing.

'But I know that carriage,' I said. 'Look!' Albert's coat of arms was just visible on the door.

'I know — I recognised the driver.' Mr King turned from me, the rain pouring around him, spattering his clothes and glistening in his hair. He called up to Tredwell, 'Where's Mr Lamont?'

'I took him to a doctor's place in Connaught Street. It was closed but he got out anyhow. He said to collect him from Miss Demeray's at nine.'

'That makes no sense!' I cried.

Tredwell shrugged. 'Those were my orders, Miss. But I confess I was worried. There was an accident in the road after I left him so I had to go another way. And then I saw him in another carriage heading for Grosvenor Crescent, only he didn't look quite the thing. I thought I must be mistaken but I can't explain it. I was that uneasy I'd just about made my mind up to turn round.'

'Quick!' said Mr King. 'Cabbie, take this for your fare. Tredwell, Grosvenor Crescent.'

We stopped near the park. Everything was in darkness, and freezing rain poured down. Under the street lamps, raindrops came down like flashes of yellow fire and fizzled into puddles of gold, but they barely made a dent in the gloom.

Tredwell took down the lantern from the carriage and we started down a pavement which ran like a river. Trees and gate posts loomed from the gardens of grand houses set back from the pavement. In almost every home, the warmth of lights seeped through the window-shutters and curtains which had been closed against the coming night. But Dovecote House was cold and dark, with dead leaves sodden and slippery on its neglected steps.

'Sir! Come quickly!' Tredwell stood shivering over a dark shape behind the gate.

It was Albert. Something darker than rain ran from his head, but when I whispered his name, he groaned. 'Where's Connie? Why didn't she wait?'

Mr King and Tredwell knelt to lift him. I slipped round to the window by which we'd entered before. It was ajar and a scrap of material flapped damply from the catch: fine linen, and lace. I climbed in and tiptoed into the hallway. Cheap candles were dotted about, their dirty yellow glow illuminating damp footprints on the tiles. Keeping my back to the walls, I followed them until I reached a door. Before I could decide what to do, it opened and a tall, hatless, huddled shape slipped out.

'Miss Fleet?' I whispered. The figure paused then whispered, 'Miss Caster?'

I stepped out of the shadow.

'Quick, we've got to get out and we're leaving footprints everywhere.'

'I know,' said Connie, 'I found a cloth to mop up as I went back. They'll never know we were here.'

Steps across the floor of the room above made us freeze. Mumbled words faded away. We breathed again.

'Come on,' I said, 'Albert's hurt.'

We tiptoed to the window, sweeping the floor as best we could and climbed back through, unhooking Connie's ripped linen from the catch. We hurried towards the men, and Mr King grabbed my shoulders. 'Where did you go?'

'I've got Connie.'

'I don't care. You should have told me first.' He pulled me into a hug.

I fought myself free. 'Let me go, what's happened to Albert?'

'He'll be all right. He's had a blow to the head, but it's not severe. We need to get him to a doctor. We'll take you to your place first and perhaps get a doctor there. It may save explanations for Tredwell.'

We walked to the carriage as briskly as possible, Tredwell and Mr King holding Albert up to help him walk.

'What happened?' I whispered to Connie.

'I arrived at the doctor's early. Albert wasn't there, but the doctor offered me tea while we waited. Something about the taste made me uneasy. I waited till Dr Bradley left the room to look for Albert, and tipped it back into the teapot. Then I pretended to be drowsy. Albert still hadn't arrived, and I suggested Dr Bradley checked in the street. I sneaked out the back way, and then went to Dovecote House. I hoped Albert would go straight there if I wasn't at the doctor's.'

She cradled his head in her lap, his blood smearing her father's coat. Her hair was half down, trailing over her shoulders. 'I lost my hat,' she said unnecessarily. 'Mother will kill me.'

'You should have waited,' groaned Albert.

'I didn't want you drugged.'

'So you got me slugged instead.'

'Shhh…' Connie stroked Albert's hair and he was silent.

With difficulty, she leaned forward to whisper in my ear.

'Tomorrow, you are taking a day's leave whether you like it or not and we are going to get to the bottom of this.' She patted her chest, which looked bulkier even than normal. 'I've got the picture. It was in what I think was the housekeeper's room. Now we've got to find out what the link to your Father is.'

I couldn't argue. Miss Gregory had no-one else.

Miss Gregory . . . why did the name ring a bell? Something in Father's papers. Something from long ago.

'Stop plotting, you two,' said Mr King.

'And,' Connie whispered even lower, 'we need a day without men making things even more complicated.'

I couldn't argue with that either.

CHAPTER 24
Connie

I smacked my forehead. How could I have been so stupid?

'Tredwell!' I shouted.

'Yes ma'am?' came the stoic reply.

'Stop at the next telegraph office, please. I have an urgent message to send.'

'Yes, ma'am.' And the carriage quickened pace.

'What is it, Connie?' asked Katherine, frowning.

'We have to move quickly,' I said. 'Dr Bradley — if he is a doctor — knows that we're on to him, and that we know the situation. He also knows my name —'

Katherine gasped.

'I know. I'm an idiot.' I turned to Mr King. 'And I'm sorry for doubting you. He made it seem so plausible.'

'You're not stupid at all. He was very convincing,' said Mr King. 'What are we going to do now?'

'I'm going to do what I should have done ages ago, if I'd been brave enough,' I said. 'I'm going to pull rank.'

***

My first wire was to our family doctor:

Medical opinion required re: lady imprisoned by servants, said to be insane. Imperative we move her to safe place. Will send carriage with Lamont coat of arms to fetch you in next hour. Do NOT board any other carriage. Regards Connie Swift.

My next wire was to a man who had terrified me up to the age of about twelve, when I had finally realised that he wasn't really going to put me in prison for swinging my legs on my chair. Chief Inspector Barnes was a red-faced man with bushy side-whiskers and a half-assumed air of ferocity. He had also been at school with Father, and was one of the few guests that Father actually sought out at dinner parties.

Dear Chief Inspector, I need you to scare someone else this time. A Miss Gregory is being imprisoned and drugged in her own home by servants. Need help to release her. Will send carriage with Lamont coat of arms to fetch you in next hour. Board NO OTHER CARRIAGE. Regards Connie Swift. PS Promise not to swing legs on chair.

I handed the forms in and slid my shillings across the counter — more money spent. I hoped fervently that this time we would succeed. This felt like my last chance.

'What now?' asked Katherine.

'We'll take Albert home and get him patched up,' I said.

Albert smiled feebly. 'Wish I could join you. Think I'd be more of a liability, though.'

'It isn't your fault,' I said. 'I'm sorry you got hurt.' I leaned down and kissed his forehead, as far from the wound as I could.

His eyes sprang open. 'Well,' he said. 'Maybe this isn't

185

so bad after all.'

'When you've quite finished,' said Katherine, nudging me, 'would you care to explain the plan?'

'Of course,' I said. 'Here's how it goes.'

***

By the time we dropped Albert off he was able to sit up and walk unaided. His sister glared at us. 'What on earth has happened to Bertie?'

'Someone attempted to rob him in the street,' said Mr King. 'He gave as good as he got, though.'

That calmed her considerably, and she led Albert away, muttering about doctors and poultices and the state of his clothes.

Our next stop was at Dr Farquhar's house in Harley Street. I felt suddenly shy as I gazed up at the impassive brown brick facade, with its unseeing windows. Was I sure?

'Come along,' said Mr King. 'I'll cover you.'

The door opened before I could press the bell. 'Well, now,' said Dr Farquhar. He already had his overcoat on. 'Would you care to tell me what this is about, Miss Connie?'

I took a deep breath, and tried to find the words. Mr King stepped forward. 'James King, journalist,' he said, offering a hand. 'Miss Swift has been assisting me with a case of false imprisonment, and your help will be invaluable.'

'I see,' Dr Farquhar's eyebrows had disappeared beneath his hat. 'Where are we heading?'

'Grosvenor Crescent.'

The doctor whistled. 'I see. One moment.' When he reappeared, he was carrying his medical bag. 'Let's be on our way.'

Chief Inspector Barnes lived in rooms in Holborn — handy for the Yard, he always declared, looking particularly stern. I could see a light, and when I rang his door-bell he answered within half a minute. 'Will I need a gun?' he asked. 'I'm assuming yes.' And he produced a shining pistol from a drawer on the hall stand. 'Bessie here always enjoys a trip out.'

I swallowed. 'That might be useful.'

Mr King held out his hand. 'James King, journ —'

'Delighted,' said the Chief Inspector, nodding. 'Now, Connie, what's going on?'

'I'll tell you in the carriage,' I said, buoyed up on a wave of gratitude. 'There's no time to lose.'

***

Chief Inspector Barnes insisted we pick up reinforcements on the way. Albert's carriage was a roomy one; but with Katherine, Mr King, Dr Farquhar, the Chief Inspector, two constables, and myself, we were a little close for comfort. Another constable was on the box with Tredwell. All in all, we were as well-equipped as we could be, yet I still felt uneasy.

Katherine felt me trembling beside her, and squeezed my hand. 'Nearly there,' she whispered.

When the carriage drew up at Dovecote House, a policeman was standing outside. I groaned. 'Look who it is.'

The Chief Inspector peered out. 'Constable,' he said, mildly. 'Is there a reason for your presence?'

The policeman saluted. 'There certainly is, sir. Persistent offenders, sir, trying to bust their way in and trouble a poor old invalid lady. They've been at it again today.'

'Have they, now.' The Chief Inspector's voice was still calm. Dangerously calm. 'Who reported it, Constable...'

'Fraser, sir,' the policeman supplied. 'The butler came out and told me. He said if it went on they'd have to move the poor dear.'

'Mm. In that case I shall call and reassure them.' He descended from the carriage. 'Judkins and Smith, you go round the back. Campbell, stay two paces to my rear. Everyone else, come with me. And you —' He swung round to address Fraser. 'Stay with the carriage.'

Constable Fraser goggled as Mr King handed Katherine and I down from the carriage. 'But sir, it's them! Those are the meddlesome ladies behind it all!'

The Chief Inspector paused. 'Really, Fraser?'

'Yes!' Fraser pointed an accusing finger.

'So the servants of the house are keeping their mistress in the attic, and you think these ladies are the problem?' Shaking his head, he ascended the steps and rang the bell.

Nothing happened.

He rang again, and footsteps hurried to the door. It opened to reveal Mr Duncan.

The Viper.

'Good evening, sir,' he said, eyeing the party gathered on the steps. 'What can I do for you?'

'I'd like to come in, please,' said the Chief Inspector.

The Viper's eyes narrowed. 'Could I ask why, please? My mistress isn't at home.'

'Aren't you going to tell him she's dead?' I asked. 'That's your usual line, isn't it?'

The Viper made to close the door, but the Chief Inspector's foot shot forward. 'I think not,' he said, quietly.

'Do you have a warrant to enter?' The Viper glanced behind him. 'It's quite all right, dear. I'll see to it.'

The Chief Inspector gave the door a shove, and it banged against the wall. 'Not now you won't.' He turned to me. 'What's his name?'

'Duncan,' I said, 'Ebenezer Duncan.'

'Well, Ebenezer Duncan, I am arresting you on suspicion of false imprisonment. Cuff him, Campbell.' The policeman strode forward, unhooking the cuffs from his belt. The Viper offered no resistance but an unpleasant glint shone in his eyes, and I wondered if he would be able to slither out of the cuffs.

The Magpie, her eyes staring, was backing away. Suddenly she ran, a blur of black and white, slamming the kitchen door. 'I'll let the men at the back see to her,' chuckled the Chief Inspector. 'Let her think she's escaped for a few seconds. Now, where did you say this lady is being kept?'

'She was in the attic,' I gasped.

'Right. Campbell, you stay here with this man, in case anyone else turns up.'

The attic stairs creaked just as before. The key was in the door. 'You two go in first,' said Dr Farquhar. 'She's seen you and might not be too distressed.'

I nudged Katherine. 'Go on. She wrote to you, first of all.'

Katherine reached out, and turned the key in the lock. She turned the knob, and the door opened.

And no-one was there. The mattress had gone, and the room was filled with tea chests and dust sheets, much like many of the other rooms.

The Chief Inspector turned to me, eyebrows raised.

'She was there!' I cried. 'She was!'

'Perhaps they moved her downstairs,' said Mr King.

We checked the other attics in case they'd moved her. Nothing. We looked in all the bedrooms, throwing off the dust sheets and peering under the beds. Nothing.

'Miss Gregory!' I shouted, and my voice rang out in the muffled rooms. 'Miss Gregory!'

'They've taken her somewhere,' muttered Katherine. 'The doctor must have moved her this afternoon, after you went to him, Connie.'

'Oh no.' I covered my face, and sank down into a chair.

'We got her, sir!' a deep voice shouted from the kitchen. 'Just cuffing her now.'

'Told you she wasn't at home,' called the Viper. I imagined his reptilian smile, and shuddered. There was no proof that any of it had ever happened, except for our word... I sobbed, unable to keep the tears from falling.

'Shhhh...' Katherine knelt beside me. 'It'll be all right, Connie, really it will.'

'How?' I whispered. 'That's it. I tried my hardest, and I failed.'

She said nothing, and my heart sank to my boots. Shocked out of crying, I lifted my head to look at her.

And then I heard it, too.

A low wail above our heads.

The Chief Inspector stiffened, like a hunting dog, then strode to the door. Dr Farquhar followed him. We ran up the stairs and threw open the doors, bawling 'Miss Gregory! Miss Gregory!'

A faint wail, from the middle attic. We stared in incomprehension at the boxes and shadows.

'We need candles,' said the Chief Inspector.

'I'll go,' said Mr King.

It seemed an age till he returned with candles and matches. The attic was silent, the air thick with dust and gloom. Even the lit candles did little to brighten it.

'She isn't behind anything,' said Dr Farquhar, clambering among a nest of chairs. 'I don't see —'

'I do,' said Katherine. 'Look.' We followed her pointing finger towards a large tea chest. It was nailed shut. 'Do you see them?'

I drew closer, and gasped. In the side of the chest were four holes, each drilled in the centre of a knot of wood. I knelt, and put my candle as close as I dared. 'I can see something…' My finger was too small to go in. I rummaged in my bag, found a pencil, and poked it into the hole.

'Aah!' A startled scream, followed by another wail, a low animal noise that chilled my blood.

'Good God,' said the Chief Inspector. He reached into his pocket, brought out a stout penknife, and inserted the blade into the small gap between lid and chest. His face went beet-red with effort, until nails squeaked and wood splintered.

The lid lifted to reveal Miss Gregory still in her nightdress, curled in the chest. Her eyes were wide, and she was shivering. 'Don't poke me again,' she said. 'Please, don't poke me again.'

'We won't,' said Dr Farquhar. 'Do you promise, Connie?'

I smiled through my tears. 'I promise.' I glanced at the Chief Inspector, and a smile flitted across his face, too.

Dr Farquhar and Mr King helped Miss Gregory out of the chest. She was stick-thin, and unable to stand without

191

help. 'Madam, you need a hot bath, a square meal, and a good night's sleep,' said the doctor. 'That's my diagnosis, before anything else.'

Miss Gregory's watery eyes gleamed. 'That sounds wonderful,' she said. Her mouth seemed to have difficulty in forming the words. 'But how? They won't let me have that here.' She looked from one to another of us, helplessly.

I wiped my tears away and stood up. 'I know where,' I said, putting a hand on Miss Gregory's long, thin forearm. 'You can come and stay at my house. We have plenty of spare rooms, and lots of food, and nice servants to take care of you.'

'But Connie —' said Katherine.

'But nothing,' I said. 'I can't possibly be in any more trouble than I am now. And she can't stay here alone, not with Dr Bradley and Miss Armitage still at large.' I turned to the Chief Inspector and Dr Farquhar. 'If you can stop Mother from killing me, I'd be very grateful.'

Both men smiled, rather uneasily.

'We'll do our best,' said the Chief Inspector.

'I can always patch up any injuries,' said Dr Farquhar.

'That'll have to do,' I said. 'Time to go, I think.' And our motley procession advanced down the stairs, past the Magpie and the Viper with their guards, and into the waiting carriage.

CHAPTER 25
Katherine

I was beyond exhausted. In a different set of circumstances I'd have enjoyed visiting Connie's home, but even shocked into near silence, her mother was terrifying.

'You ought to be very proud of your daughter, Euphemia,' said Chief Inspector Barnes, beaming down at Connie's mother as if she was a simpering girl but, I noticed, clenching his clasped hands behind his back. 'She and Miss Demeray have doubtless saved a life tonight.'

Mrs Swift's glare could have turned a blancmange to stone. I resisted the urge to cower and realised my legs were swinging from the tall, hard, high-backed chair she had assigned me. I sat rigid.

'Benson!' she called. 'Bring a mop. Miss Demeray is dripping on the parquet.'

Connie returned from delivering Miss Gregory to Mary. She looked even more tired than I felt. But perhaps she thought the same about me. She had done her best to re-pin her hair but sodden rat's-tails stuck to her cheeks. Her father's coat was grubby and bloodstained, and a rip in her hem revealed the gap where a piece of her petticoat had been torn off. She flung herself in another chair and closed her eyes.

'Constance, sit up straight.'

It was impossible not to follow the order myself, though I was not the one being addressed. I tucked my feet in their ruined shoes well under my skirts and dropped my eyes.

'One is used to new visitors handing in cards,' said Mrs Swift. 'And having the courtesy not to arrive at dinner time.'

'For pity's sake, Mother,' said Connie and slumped back.

Mrs Swift's mouth dropped open.

'This is hardly a social call, Euphemia,' said the Chief Inspector. 'I repeat, these young ladies saved a life tonight. And we need their help to apprehend two dangerous criminals. I think they could do with a stiff brandy.'

'What they need is a good smacking,' said Mrs Swift. 'They have been running around like strumpets.'

'And exactly how do you know so much about strumpets, Mother?' snapped Connie.

Mrs Swift gasped. Even the Chief Inspector gasped. I saw Mr King's grin and turned my nervous laugh into a cough. My legs started swinging again.

'Constance! How dare you? I have given you all the…'

'Advantages in life,' snarled Connie, 'Yes I know. You have sheltered me from the evils of the wide world, you have introduced me to the best people in the best circles…'

'And this is how you repay me? Mixing with messenger boys and policemen…'

The Chief Inspector coughed.

'I don't mean you Ernest, I mean *uniformed* persons.' She might as well have said 'diseased'. She drew herself up to her full height and gave her daughter a look which should have frizzled her to cinders. 'You have cavorted with an undisciplined girl who needs the direction of a good man...'

I wondered who she meant and then caught Mr King's twinkling eye. Me? Undisciplined? When I did eight hours of typing a day. When I'd managed to pay the bills and keep the house going for three years. Needing a good man? I'd managed perfectly well without any sort of man. Really. How rude. I glared straight back at her.

'You have,' Mrs Swift continued, 'and I can't believe I am saying this — you have burgled a house. You have interfered in matters which are none of your business, and furthermore you have ruined a coat and a petticoat, lost a hat and are sitting before me like a . . . like a...'

I thought Connie would stand up. She was at least three inches taller than her mother but she sat back, pursed her lips and steepled her fingers. While her mother's voice had risen higher and louder, Connie's was low and calm.

'I am sitting before you like someone who has a point to her existence. You gave me parties and dinners, parading me as if I were ready for market. No, don't interrupt. You introduced me to girls from the best families, provided they had eligible brothers and cousins and even, on one occasion, a widowed father. What you never asked was "Are you happy, Constance? Who is your greatest friend?" In fact, you never even troubled to find out if I had a friend at all.'

Now Connie stood up. She could have glared into her

195

mother's face and jabbed a finger, but she didn't. She simply stood like a queen and looked down her nose. Then she waved her arm towards the upper floors where Miss Gregory was being cosseted, then to Mr King, and finally to me.

'Well, Mother,' she said, 'I wasn't happy and I had no friends. I only knew people who were nice to my face and laughed behind my back. I barely felt I deserved to exist. But these last two weeks have taught me that I can be useful and I've found friends. Real friends. People who simply like and value me for myself.' As our eyes met, I saw a chink of the Connie I'd met in that restaurant, uncertain, worried, trying to make herself look small. And I remembered myself, small and irritable, defensive, miserable. I smiled, rose and stood by her side. We faced her mother together.

'And what's more, Mother,' said Connie, 'I shall make my own mind up about a husband, if and when I find one I like. So please stop parading me and concentrate on polishing up the others. In the meantime, if I wish to cavort like a strumpet I will. Although since I don't know how and you do, perhaps you could teach me.'

Mrs Swift went purple and swept out of the room.

The Chief Inspector relaxed a little, 'Miss Demeray, I have sent an officer round to put your aunt's mind at rest, and you've told me all you can. I shall send you home in the care of Mr King and one of my officers. Assuming, that is, neither you nor your aunt have any objection.'

What felt like a year ago, Mr King had held me tight. Aunt Alice would have been scandalised, but it had been the embrace of a terrified friend and nothing more. I shook my head.

'Can I come too?' said Connie, 'I need to cool down a little, and probably so does Mother.'

Frenzied banging sounded at the door, and as we were gathering our things Albert burst in on us. He was pale and his head was bandaged, but he looked like a knight on a quest.

'I had to make sure it wasn't a dream,' he said. 'I had to make sure you were all right.' He gazed at Connie, bedraggled as she was, as if she were a Greek sculpture. Then he turned to me and grimaced. 'How do K, you look rather a mess.'

***

The rain had slowed a little, but the roads were slick and fallen leaves sliming under our wheels didn't help. A number of collisions on the normal route meant we had to take a different one, and we drove down darkened streets towards the Embankment, the horses' hooves and wheels splashing through puddles and potholes. Unable to get much wetter, I put my head out of the window. Ahead, the lamps along the river's edge were beautiful, like a string of fairy lanterns above the turgid waters of the Thames. A movement in a narrow side-street caught my eye. Two people were arguing as they walked in the shadows of the tall buildings. A slim woman, a man of good height and bearing. Far from the woman pleading with the man, it was the other way about. The man was pulling on the woman's arm, while she was shaking him off and increasing her pace. I prodded Connie, who was lolling half-asleep against Albert.

'Miss Armitage?' I said.

'Yes, I think so,' she said, 'and isn't that Dr Bradley?'

Mr King pulled me back and looked outside, then

leaned out of the other window and whispered to the driver. Our carriage sped up, turned a corner and tucked into the shadows as best it could.

We climbed out.

'We've got to catch them,' said Mr King. 'They're heading for the Embankment, and from there they can escape easily. You girls stay in the carriage with Lamont, and the officer and I shall —'

'Do we have to have this conversation again?' I said.

'You're not going anywhere without me either,' said Albert.

'But you're injured,' argued Connie.

'It's just a biff. I grew up with a bunch of older brothers, a sister, and K knocking me about. I'll be fine.'

'In that case, you and Miss Swift take the policeman and go that way,' said Mr King, 'Miss Demeray and I shall go that way. Hopefully we can trap them in the middle...'

The others slipped away, leaving me and Mr King to walk swiftly but quietly in a slightly different direction. But Miss Armitage and Dr Bradley had changed routes too. They were coming towards us. Mr King led me to a doorway and whispered in my ear.

'Miss Demeray, we can't tackle them on our own, and if they see who we are, they'll run. If we let them pass, we can follow them and make sure they can't double back when they see the policeman. But we can't let them see us now. I'm sorry to have to suggest this, but do you mind if we pretend to kiss? No-one looks directly at kissing people.'

His arms encircled me, but a gap remained between us. It was ridiculous. He probably looked as if he was going to dance with me. And then they'd be bound to stare. I flung my arms round his neck and pulled him closer. I felt the warmth of his body through our damp clothes, one hand in the small of my back, the other across my shoulders. His moustache tickled my lips at first but his mouth was soft and sweet, and for a few seconds I forgot everything but that. Footsteps passed. Urgent voices spoke.

'You mustn't ever tell,' Dr Bradley muttered.

'I will if they catch me.' Miss Armitage's voice was louder, as if she didn't care who heard.

'You mustn't. I shall be ruined!'

'Likely you're ruined anyway. You helped us drug her. The death certificate is there, in your handwriting, just waiting for the date.'

'Yes, but you're the one who attacked an innocent Army officer.'

'If he was innocent, why was he trying to send black tulips to that girl?'

'I'll not be ruined by a housekeeper!'

'Like that now, is it? After all you promised me! We'll see.'

The footsteps quickened, the voices faded and Mr King let me go. He looked down at me and I could make out raised eyebrows.

'If you're going to pretend,' I said, 'you have to do it properly.'

He cleared his throat. 'If we're ever forced to pretend again, can you stand on a higher step? I think I've cricked my neck.'

He sidestepped my kick.

We stepped out of the doorway and walked briskly after Miss Armitage and Dr Bradley. As we neared the Embankment, the others stepped out of the shadows to cut them off. With a squeal, Miss Armitage ran. Dr Bradley paused and then rushed after her. They dashed through the traffic on the main road, with us trapped on the other side. Within moments they would catch a cab to who knew where. But Miss Armitage seemed to be wavering. She stared at us, then at the policeman, who was blowing his whistle and trying to stop the traffic.

'Give yourselves up!' the policeman shouted, 'It'll go better for you if you do.'

Dr Bradley was tugging at Miss Armitage, and she was trying to free herself, striking out at him. Passers-by ignored them at first, then backed away and stared as they fought. Miss Armitage kicked and struggled but she had little chance against Dr Bradley, who towered over her. He had pinioned her arms and was dragging her towards the wall.

The policeman ran across the road, but before he could get to them Dr Bradley pulled Miss Armitage over the parapet and into the Thames.

It was high tide.

CHAPTER 26
Connie

'I know it's in here somewhere,' said Katherine, pulling yet another bundle of letters from what seemed to be a bottomless drawer in her father's study.

'How can you be so sure?' I looked about us. Every flat surface, and some that weren't, was strewn with papers, covered with ink in every colour, and handwriting of every style.

'When Reg said *Gregory*, something clicked in my head. I remember coming to fetch Father for lunch, and he laid down a letter which he had been studying. "An elegant puzzle," he said, "but not sufficient to keep me from a meal."'

'He sounds very sensible,' I observed. We had been shut up in the study so long that I was convinced we had missed at least one meal. 'Although his filing system leaves something to be desired.'

'Henry did wonders,' said Katherine, quietly. 'But there were always more exciting things to be getting on with.'

She undid the string binding the letters, and spread the envelopes out, checking the postmarks. 'No . . . no . . . no . . . no...' She sighed, and returned to the task.

I bent and retrieved another bundle of letters, and did the same. It was almost therapeutic after the whirl and fury we had been through, and we were both still in the process of winding down, like a pair of overtaxed pocket-watches.

Miss Armitage and Dr Bradley had never surfaced from the Thames. When they were dragged from the river, the doctor's arms encircled Miss Armitage in a macabre embrace. The weight of her sodden dress and petticoats had probably dragged them both to their doom; and in making sure she would never tell, Bradley had sealed his own death-warrant.

When Chief Inspector Barnes called, he told us that the Viper refused to talk, sitting silent and resolute while questions rebounded from him. The Magpie, however, said enough for two, spilling detail upon detail until the pair were bound in guilt. 'She will be treated with a degree of leniency,' remarked the Chief Inspector. 'Her esteemed spouse...' He shook his head.

While Chief Inspector Barnes would not share the details, he confirmed Reg's account. Miss Gregory had spoken of her search for a family treasure to Miss Armitage — or Gart, as the Magpie called her — and the group determined that they would do their best to get a share of it. Their efforts increased the more secretive Miss Gregory grew, to the point where she accused them of trying to steal from her — and at that point, her captivity began. 'The more I hear,' the Chief Inspector said, ramming tobacco savagely into his pipe, 'the gladder I am that you two took matters into your own hands.'

My mother was less glad. Not only had I interrupted dinner and ruined a perfectly good set of clothes — never mind running away in the middle of the night — but I had also brought her an unexpected and (she intimated) unsavoury house guest. However, the Chief Inspector took Father for a chat in the study, after which Miss Gregory's convalescence was at least tolerated, if not actively welcomed. Mother's discovery that the name Gregory featured in *Debrett's* also did much to reconcile her to the new lodger.

Miss Gregory's recovery was aided by the presence of Maria, who had turned up on our doorstep the second she heard the news. Miss Gregory re-engaged her on the spot, and Maria bustled around the room with the step of a woman twenty years younger. Reg and his sister came too, and a few days later Miss Gregory was able, under the care of Dr Farquhar, to return to Dovecote House. Katherine and I accompanied her, and I had to turn away more than once as Miss Gregory stared in incomprehension at the sheeted furniture, the dusty rooms, and the many filled-in holes in the garden. 'They never found it, did they?' she faltered.

'They can't have done, ma'am,' said Maria grimly, 'or they'd have vanished with it.'

I was brought back to the study by a shriek. Katherine was staring at an envelope. 'I know that writing!' she cried. 'But look how much clearer it is.'

She fumbled the letter from its envelope, and we read:

Dear Mr Demeray,
I am so terribly afraid that a mishap will befall these that I am entrusting them to you. One is an old painting

and the other I found in a dusty old book. I know the painting by heart, and I keep the commonplace book I found with the original of this verse very close; but I still fear, not close enough.

I send you this copy so that if anything happens to me, you may be able to solve the mystery which has plagued me for so many years. It does, I believe, relate to some wealth my father always said was missing.

Mr Demeray — Roderick — I know it is many years since we lost acquaintance with each other. But I am sure I remember you, when we were children, persuading me to dig in the garden to find it? Our nurses were so angry at the mud on our clothes, especially mine. I suspect that was your first adventure. Of course, we had nothing but a half-remembered family story to guide us. However, a few years ago I found this poem, written in the old way. It was difficult to read, but I believe I have transcribed it correctly.

Where oft the dancing feet may go
Twixt dragon's breath and moonbeam's glow
Se'en faerie steps away from dawn
You'll find the stone that faces morn
Seek tulips black in midnight wood
From midst must follow strait most good
From flow'r in shade to shadow flow'r
Fall arrow-like at southern hour
And from their dull, cold, hard disguise
Treasures phoenix-like will arise.

It seems quite mystical, with dragons and black tulips, and I wonder if the answer lies far afield. If you can make anything of these, please write by return.

Yours in hope,
Thirza Gregory

Katherine sighed. 'I imagine this got buried under the rest of Father's correspondence. I certainly don't remember him mentioning it again.'

'I wonder which painting she's talking ab —' I stopped and stared at Katherine, who was doing exactly the same. Her expression, though, had an undercurrent of horror.

'And I sold the painting to Miss Armitage!' she whispered.

'How could we have known, though?' I glanced down at the letter with its flowing, old-fashioned hand. 'Not that I feel I know much more now. I can see why no-one's found the treasure.'

Katherine slid the letter into its envelope. Her eyes gleamed with determination. 'Connie, where did you put the tulip painting?'

'In the safe, at home,' I said. 'Do you think Miss Gregory's up to this?'

Katherine shrugged, and I could see the fire in her dimming a little bit. 'It can't hurt to try,' she said. 'And I can't miss work much longer.' Her eyes fell. Her face said what her voice would not: *we can't afford it.*

I would have given her the dress off my back to get her out of that wretched job — but I knew she would never accept it. 'Then let's go,' I said. 'We can pick up Albert and Mr King on the way.'

***

Dovecote House was already much improved. Maria and her family were working room by room to bring it back to life, in the intervals of caring for Miss Gregory. We found her in a small, pretty sitting-room, her sofa illuminated by the warm afternoon sun.

'Hello,' she said, turning her head to look at us. 'So nice to see welcome faces, after all these years.'

We introduced the topic as gently as we could, and put the letter before her. A faint smile lit her features as she read the lines. 'Well, now.' She sighed. 'I spent so long finding out about fairy rings, and folklore, and the possibility of black tulips, and ancient woodlands... And I can barely remember any of it. Such a waste.' Her wrinkled hand clenched into a fist.

'Do you remember this painting, Miss Gregory?' I asked. Connie unwrapped it and held the tulips up for her inspection.

She chuckled and reached out for it, tracing the tulips with a finger. 'I never thought I would see this again! Oh, the hours I spent staring at this. I grew to hate it, but now... Now I'm rather pleased to see it.'

'Do you know what the family treasure was, Miss Gregory?' asked Mr King.

She shook her head. 'Everything I know, and there isn't much, came to me in bits and pieces. Something my grandmother told me, or a story from the housekeeper, or this rhyme, which I found in a commonplace book my great-grandfather kept. The more I think about it, the more I wonder if it was all just —' She looked down at her hands, clasped on a quilt. 'Just a patchwork I put together because I wanted it to be true.' She blinked, and I could see wetness in her eyes.

'Shall we go and put this painting back in its place?' I asked, to distract her.

'What a good idea,' she said, grimly.

With help from Maria and Reg, Miss Gregory led us to a square, low-ceilinged room. 'It goes there,' she said, pointing to a picture of a curly-headed, velvet-clad boy playing with a puppy.

'But there's already a painting there,' said Albert.

'Yes. I moved it to replace the one I sent to your father,' she said to Katherine. 'It's much nicer. But now I would like everything back the way it was.'

Albert reached up and unhooked the painting of the child, and we saw a faint outline of paler colour on the uneven wall. He hung the tulips, and we stepped back to admire the effect.

The room was much colder than Miss Gregory's room, and I shivered. Then again, if it was little-used, they wouldn't bother lighting a fire… It took me a few moments to realise that they couldn't have lit a fire if they had wanted to. There was no fireplace. 'What do you use this room for?' I asked.

'Oh, this is just an anteroom,' Miss Gregory said, vaguely. 'It's part of the old house. The next room's much nicer.'

We passed through the doorway and stared at the oak panelling and the hammer-beam roof. This room had a vast fireplace which seemed too big for it. 'I know what you're thinking.' Miss Gregory laughed. 'My grandmother told me that this used to be the great hall, and they held parties and gatherings in here. They made it smaller and got a few extra rooms out of it when the family fortunes fell.'

'I've been in 'ere,' Reg said suddenly. 'Look!' He led us to a picture and ran his fingers along the ebony frame. 'D'you see?' There, under his hand, were the tulips we had seen in his rubbing. 'And I know them carvings on the

207

fireplace, too.'

'Your family really liked tulips, Miss Gregory,' said Mr King, looking around him.

'Sssh!'

We stared at Katherine, who was studying the letter. 'Don't you see?'

'Um, no, K,' said Albert.

Her smile lit the room. 'Dancing feet, and two sets of black tulips!'

'I'm not following,' said Mr King.

She began to walk, reading. '"Where oft the dancing feet may go" — that's this room, when it was all one room. No idea about the dragon's breath —'

'Unless they mean the big fireplace,' I joked.

Everyone goggled at me.

'Between the fireplace and the moonbeam's glow —'

'The window!' cried Albert. 'But —'

We looked up at the small, high windows.

'There's a bigger window in that room,' said Katherine, waving a hand at the room we had entered from. 'Maybe they mean that. Anyway, "Seek tulips black in midnight wood" — done!'

Miss Gregory shook her head. 'To think of the hours I spent...' But she was smiling.

'"From midst must follow strait..."' Katherine walked in a straight line from the picture. 'Now what?'

I hurried to her side and read. '"From flow'r in shade . . . to shadow flow'r" — It's the other painting! Our painting!' I ran into the other room and paced the distance from the window wall to the painting. 'Seven steps!' I shouted as I ran, and measured the distance in the great hall. 'I'm coming! Walk to meet me!'

Katherine and I met in the centre of the room. "'Fall arrow-like at southern hour…'" We gazed at the threadbare carpet. 'What's beneath this, please?'

Miss Gregory hurried to join us. 'Flagstones!' she cried, clasping her hands. 'Let's take the carpet up!'

Reg, Mr King and Albert moved the furniture and rolled the carpet back to reveal first rush matting, then slabs of stone laid every which way. Katherine stood firm as the increasing roll advanced, hopping over it. Miss Gregory retreated, her hands to her mouth.

'Would you like a chair, ma'am?' asked Maria, but she shook her head violently.

We examined the stone on which Katherine was standing. It was firmly bedded in with its fellows, and looked as if it had never shifted since it had been laid.

'Crowbar,' said Reg. 'I'll try the shed.' He ran from the room, and we all exchanged glances. Albert moved to stand with me, and Mr King went to Katherine. Her whole face said *What if…?*

''Ere we are! Stand back everyone!' Reg tried to get the crowbar under the stone, but it was too firmly fixed.

Mr King rummaged in his pockets and produced a pocket-knife, then knelt to chip at the mortar. 'Good idea,' said Albert, doing the same. They worked silently, until one side of the stone showed a gap.

'I'm goin' in,' said Reg. He inserted the crowbar, and heaved.

The stone stayed put.

'Come on, Lamont,' said Mr King, and they added their weight to the task.

A squeak, and it lifted. Katherine and I rushed to see what had been revealed as they lifted the stone and set it aside.

Underneath was earth. 'This can't be it!' cried Katherine. 'We can't be wrong!' She knelt, plunged her hands into the soil and pushed it aside, like a terrier after a bone, leaning further and further into the hole.

'Steady, K,' called Albert.

'Aah!' she screamed, and fell forward, her arms buried up to the elbows.

'Are you all right?' I cried, lifting her out.

She raised her head. 'My hands were resting on something. It wasn't earth, or stone.'

'A spade,' said Reg on his way to the door, 'an' a bucket.'

Five minutes later, we stood in a circle, gazing at a small metal-bound chest. 'Who's gonna lift it out?' asked Reg.

We all looked at each other, then at Miss Gregory. 'I think I need to sit down,' she said faintly.

'That's a good idea,' said Katherine. 'We'll get it out, and bring it to you to open.'

Albert and Mr King lifted the chest and placed it on a table. Albert dusted it with his handkerchief. 'It has a lock,' he observed, 'but I daresay Reg can break that with his crowbar.'

Reg stepped forward, grinning.

Maria placed a chair for her mistress. We hung back, uncertain of the correct etiquette. What *should* you do when someone is opening a chest of buried treasure in front of you? I was pretty sure even *Debrett's* wouldn't have the answer to that.

'Well, come on then,' said Miss Gregory, putting her hands on the lid. 'Don't you want to see?' And it would have been rude then *not* to crowd round.

She lifted the lid, and revealed —

Dull, worn leather pouches, sitting on a dragon's hoard of golden coins.

Miss Gregory picked up a coin and peered at it. 'Spanish gold!' she breathed.

I reached for Katherine's hand, and squeezed it.

'What's in the pouches?' she asked, and her voice cracked.

'I don't know,' said Miss Gregory, grinning in a most unladylike way, 'but I intend to find out. Everyone take a pouch, and we'll see.'

'On the count of three,' said Mr King. 'One, two —'

It was like Christmas. Heavy golden chains and intricate rings set with pearls, cabochons, peridots and garnets. '"Treasures phoenix-like..."' whispered Katherine, turning a necklace this way and that to catch the light.

A high-pitched laugh made us turn to Miss Gregory. 'So many years,' she choked out, 'to find so much wealth, and I don't even need it!'

I saw Katherine's gaze fix on the necklace. 'If you don't want it —'

'I'm sorry, dear,' said Miss Gregory. 'I didn't mean to sound ungrateful. What I'm trying to say — I think — is that while this is wonderful, and I'm so glad you found it, all this —' She reached into the box and let the coins trickle through her fingers. 'This isn't important. The important thing is that you've set me free. From those horrible people, yes, and from my own ridiculous self-imposed quest.' She took her hands out of the chest. 'Let's put it away for now.'

211

We returned the jewels to the chest, and Miss Gregory closed the lid, then gazed at us all in turn. 'If you could help me just a little more,' she said. 'I must telegraph my solicitor, and the bank. For the first time in a long time, I have something important to do.'

Chapter 27
Katherine

I woke with tears in my eyes. From beyond the curtains came the dawn chorus: the chirruping, arguing, flirting sound of spring.

The events in November seemed a long time ago. I threw back the covers, trying to recall the dream. It had all but gone. I just had an image of my chaotic, disorganised father laid out neat and still, and of calm, ordered Henry in a tangle of broken limbs. It was exactly four years to the day that they had left for Constantinople, and the only word I'd received since their arrival had come yesterday in a damaged, dirty envelope.

'Sorry, Miss Demeray,' the postman said. 'It took a while to work out who it was for, but the Royal Mail prides itself on delivering eventually.'

Eventually. It was three years old, dated shortly after they had disappeared, at about the time I was settling into my job at the Department. Father's letter to the family was, as usual, like notes for a lecture, full of local colour, half finished anecdotes, recipes, sketches. Its tone was strained however, with too many loose ends, as if he wrote to reassure himself more than the family awaiting his return. Enclosed was a brief note from Henry, addressed to me.

My dear Katherine, he wrote, *I fear I may have misled you when we last spoke. I do not wish you to feel in any way tied to me. I apologise for any misunderstanding. Should I return, I shall speak more frankly, but in the meantime, I remain your obedient and affectionate servant, Henry.*

What did it mean? Had he fallen in love with someone else? Or had the hints and whispers we shared meant nothing? The kiss on my cheek, the hand held a little too long — were they just small flirtations? I had nothing to compare with it and no-one to ask. Or was he simply telling me not to wait because he feared they would not come back?

I made myself ready to face the world. I couldn't tell anyone about Henry's words. Even thinking about them made me blush. I couldn't work out how I felt. On the one hand I felt humiliated, and on the other relieved. I had a feeling I was no longer the serious, predictable girl he had made vague promises to. And the thought of a serious, predictable life no longer appealed to me. Going to work had cured me of that. And as for a sensible, organised husband...

Still, today was Saturday and a different sort of adventure was afoot.

By the time we'd finished our rushed breakfast, my mood had recovered. It was impossible not to be caught up in the excitement. I was wearing the lovely jacket Aunt

214

Alice had made for me with the off-cuts of Connie's blue dress. I had taken a morning's leave, the spring sun was blazing and we were taking Aunt Alice cycling for the third time.

'It'll be the death of you all,' muttered Ada, as she cleared the table, 'you mark my words. Death or dishonour. Gallivanting. It's not right. And I'm telling you, Gallivanting leads to Shenanigans as sure as my name's Ada Jones.'

'You should come too, Ada,' said Margaret.

'I'd as soon run naked down the lane,' said Ada, 'which is near enough what you're doing, Miss Margaret. Showing your legs like a trollop. I'd give notice, I'm that ashamed. But then I heard Elsie's young mistress is doing the same. The world is going mad.'

Margaret was resplendent in tweed cycling knickerbockers. There was almost as much material in them as in my skirt, so it was hard to make out her legs specifically, although admittedly her gaiters revealed the shape of her slim calves and ankles. I was fairly sure no-one had realised my skirt was a divided one. It was useful having the right contacts at last.

'Now then, Ada.' said Aunt Alice, 'Once the young men started coming round with bicycles of their own, someone had to chaperone Albert and Miss Swift. And you know Katherine and Mr King wouldn't take it seriously.'

'Shenanigans,' muttered Ada.

Aunt Alice continued. 'And while Miss Robson offered to chaperone, it's not fair to expect her to do it all herself, is it? Especially since someone sent Margaret and me bicycles too. It's good exercise and very sociable.'

She blushed, and Miss Robson smothered a grin.

Connie and Albert weren't the only ones needing to be chaperoned. A gentleman, with a moustache so magnificent it made Mr King's look like a trainee, had taken a shine to Aunt Alice the moment she joined the cycling club. To my surprise, it turned out to be Major Fairbank, into whom the attack in November seemed to have knocked some sense, as he was now flirting with women ten years younger than himself rather than thirty.

The Major was regaling Aunt Alice with the story of his attack for perhaps the four hundredth time.

'And there I was, Miss Perry, villainously assaulted in broad daylight. Let me tell you, dear lady, I would never have been taken off guard if I hadn't been momentarily blinded as I came from the florist's shop. Those monstrous brigands came out of the sun like the cowards they were when I had simply been humouring a child who had a fancy for black tulips. Why they attacked me I still do not know. After all, it was not as if Miss Swift had anything to do with uncovering the villains, other than having met Mr Lamont at the Frobishers' dinner party.'

'Oh dear, Major,' said Aunt Alice for the four hundredth time, 'I do hope you are not still suffering.'

'A soldier has a head of iron,' he responded without irony. Aunt Alice, whom I had found reading a transcript of The Viper's trial, smiled her gentle smile and said nothing about the fact that the evidence given was that the Major had been felled by a thin woman with an umbrella.

'Oh Major, how thrilling!' exclaimed Mrs MacClean, a widow of around forty.

As Aunt Alice let them fall back, her bicycle started to wobble. Serious Mr Frampton rushed over to help improve her technique.

'Like this, Miss Perry,' he murmured, riding closer to steady her handlebars while also managing his own. It seemed impossible that Aunt Alice might have done it on purpose.

It was easy to outstrip them all when we went out into the countryside. While Margaret went off with her schoolfriends, Aunt Alice seemed quite happy to leave Albert and Connie, Mr King and me under the indifferent supervision of Miss Robson. And Miss Robson appeared far more interested in chatting to her friends than supervising us.

Once we were out of sight, we slipped down a lane and slowed our pace. Albert and Connie stopped at a gate to admire the view of the outskirts of London. It was sparkling and beautiful, streams of smoke from a million chimneys drifting into the blue sky. Albert's arm sneaked round Connie's waist and she raised her face to his. For a few seconds they gazed into each other's eyes and then they kissed. They would soon be at risk of suffocation but they didn't seem to mind. Connie's hat fell off and her hair came down in thick dark blonde waves over her shoulders.

I left them to it. I was reasonably sure Albert wasn't planning any Shenanigans beyond kissing just yet, and if he was, I didn't wish to witness it. Mr King passed me with his arms crossed and his feet off the pedals, then regained control of the bicycle, turned and sped straight at me, daring me to dodge first. We had been through this before, so I ignored him and kept pedalling till I found another gate as far away from the love-birds as possible. I dismounted the bicycle and sat on the top of the gate. It was a lovely day. The sort of day when you wonder why anyone would want to live anywhere else or travel the world to search for a beauty which you could find right in front of you at home.

Mr King leant his arms on the gate and looked up at me.

'Is this what's it's like being you? Staring up at people all the time? Be careful the thin air up there doesn't make you swoon. You're not used to it.'

'Ha, ha. I suppose you think all women faint into your arms at the drop of a hat.'

'One doesn't like to boast. By the way, interesting skirt.'

I glanced down at him, and he winked.

'You forget I'm an investigator. One of Maria's creations?'

I grinned. 'Yes.'

Miss Gregory had made an incredible recovery, all things considered. Her imprisonment and sustained drugging had left her anxious, and her childhood home made her uneasy. She had sold it to a young man of means, and moved to a much smaller house which required a great deal less upkeep. Maria, with her damaged arm, could do simple cooking but little of the actual housework so Miss Gregory had hired a maid for Maria to train, and also invested some of her riches in a small workshop where Maria could train girls in dress-making using her own designs.

'I do wish Miss Gregory could have rewarded you sufficiently to give up work,' said Mr King. 'Not that there's anything wrong with you working, but you'd be easier to visit if you weren't.'

'She rewarded us all, remember. Equal shares, which is quite good considering that according to the papers all the work was done by you and Albert, while Connie and I swooned at your magnificence from a distance.'

'I did my best to get it reported accurately, but the press don't like women getting above themselves. Even short ones.' He dodged my kick. 'I was comfortable without Miss Gregory's help, and Connie and Albert need more money like spiders need more legs.'

I shrugged. Perhaps my pride would have got in the way of accepting a reward which would have allowed me to give up paid employment. I suspected it might have. At least this way it was fair. And besides…

'Miss Demeray,' said Mr King. 'I…'

'It doesn't matter. There's enough for us. Anyway, I haven't told you my news,' I said, pulling myself together. 'I've been offered a different job.'

He sighed. 'A promotion? You'll make a good…'

'No. It is an entirely different job. I'd have to leave the Department. I'd still type but…'

'Yes?'

'The same pay but only three days a week, whichever days I choose, and able to take time off with negligible notice. Paid leave to boot.'

Mr King gaped. I grinned.

'If it wasn't for the typing, I'd be worried,' he said. 'Put me out of my misery. Who's offered you the job?'

'Dr Farquhar.'

'Who?

'Connie's doctor. The one who helped us with Miss Gregory. He approached me through her the other week.'

'I'm sorry, I don't follow. You're not going to be a nurse are you? I can't imagine your bedside manner is quite the thing.'

'No, it's to write up his memoirs and also, he said,

perhaps to listen to people with problems and take notes.'

'Medical problems?'

'No. He says people tell him all sorts of things because they don't know where else to go. His words were "you like puzzles, perhaps you could work them out."' I didn't tell Mr King what the doctor had added. 'Perhaps your friend Miss Swift could help. She'll want something to do when her mother starts matchmaking again.'

'Puzzles?'

'Yes. What do you think?'

'Would you listen to what I think?'

'I might.' I breathed deep of the warm air and closed my eyes.

A few moments passed before he spoke. 'You seem a little distant today.'

'I have things on my mind.'

'Things you could tell a friend?'

I felt my face go hot. Henry's words burned in my thoughts. I tried to recall what he had actually said all that time ago when he kissed my cheek and held my hand. It hadn't been much of a kiss, really. Or hand-holding, come to that. Not that I had a great deal to go on, but Connie and Albert's closeness seemed completely different to the polite, unemotional experience I recalled.

I took a deep breath. 'Mr King, can I ask you something rather personal?' I felt my face heat up.

'Go on,' he said, looking puzzled.

'If you cared for someone, how would you kiss them? No-one has ever kissed me the way Albert kisses Connie, and I don't know if anyone has ever loved me the way that Albert loves her or whether...'

I felt myself becoming incoherent and stared out over

the countryside. I could hear nothing but bird song and my own blood in my ears. I should learn to keep my mouth shut. After about a million years, Mr King spoke. 'Well, you caught me unawares, or I'd have done a better job.'

I looked down, startled. 'I'm sorry, I don't understand.'

'I mean,' Mr King continued, 'if I'd known you were going to kiss me in that doorway, I'd have been better prepared. And then you stopped before I could display my full potential. You didn't get the opportunity to experience my expertise.'

It was my turn to gape.

'It was only a pretend kiss,' I said.

'If you say so.' He prodded me in the waist.

I leaned over to prod him back but he moved sideways. I unbalanced and he pulled me off the gate. I found myself held tight against him, looking into his face and wondering what to do next.

'May I call you Katherine?' he said. I swear I could feel his heart beating louder than my own. His face showed a nervousness I'd never seen before. 'And won't you call me James? Surely even a pretend kiss deserves a first name.'

I nodded.

'And just in case any of these "puzzles" you're taking on ever need any more "pretending", perhaps a little more practice is in order.'

His arms still held me tight, and I still didn't know what to do.

But James did.

HISTORICAL NOTE

Neither of us is a historian, but we're both interested in history and in particular the role of ordinary women.

Britain went through huge change during the sixty-four years of Queen Victoria's reign. Populations moved from country to city and London swallowed up hamlets and villages. As canals were superseded by railways, public transport links opened up, and people could travel far and wide, to find new opportunities or even to escape. Omnibuses and the underground enabled workers living on the outskirts of London to work in the centre of the city. Better communications by post, telegraph and eventually, for some, the telephone, meant that the pace of life was speeding up. And affordable bicycles meant that young people could get away from constant parental supervision.

The role of women altered as educational opportunities improved (albeit very slowly), to the point that by the end of the century women could attend university and even obtain a degree. This meant that more options became available to them. Their best bet for wealth might still be matrimony but it was becoming possible to forge a career.

The civil service, for example, found that it was more beneficial to employ educated middle-class women than less-educated working-class boys for certain roles, ultimately leading to promotion. And with teaching, office jobs and shop jobs came a kind of freedom for women that perhaps didn't exist for servants, factory workers or governesses. For all her complaints, does Katherine really think she'd prefer to sit at home sewing and waiting for someone to call? We'll have to see.

We wanted to write about what could happen if two young Victorian women decided to have an adventure, rather than write a history book, but we hope that we've captured the essence of what Connie and Katherine's world might have been like — even if we may have taken a few liberties here and there.

Having spent many happy hours on internet and library research, we'd particularly like to acknowledge the following:

How to Be a Victorian by Ruth Goodman (Viking)

'Women in the Civil Service - History': http://www.civilservant.org.uk/women-history.html

And if you want to know about the revolutionary impact of the bicycle:

'Ladies Cycling Clubs: The Politics of Victorian Women's Bicycling Associations' by Sheila Hanlon: http://www.sheilahanlon.com/?p=1889

'A List of Don'ts for Women on Bicycles Circa 1895': https://www.brainpickings.org/2012/01/03/donts-for-women-on-bicycles-1895/

Acknowledgements

First of all we would like to thank our beta readers — Ruth Cunliffe, Christine Downes, Patricia Harmon, Stephen Lenhardt, and Val Portelli — and our super speedy proofreader, John Croall. As usual, they have done a wonderful job, and we tip our top hats and raise our parasols to you all!

Our thanks also go to the members of the Facebook Cozy and Traditional Mystery Writers group for their help with the hardest part of the process — getting the book blurb into shape!

We'd also like to thank the internet and Google Docs in particular, for making the co-writing process a great deal easier. Editing's much more fun when you can send rude comments to your co-writer instantly . . . and yes, all were resolved!

Our final thanks go to you, the reader. We hope you've enjoyed Connie and Katherine's first adventure, and if you have, please would you leave us a short review on Amazon or Goodreads? Reviews are important for indie authors like us, and we'd really appreciate your feedback.

Font and Image Credits

Fonts:

Main cover font: Birmingham Titling by Paul Lloyd (freeware):
https://www.fontzillion.com/fonts/paul-lloyd/birmingham

Classic font: Libre Baskerville Italic by Impallari Type (http://www.impallari.com):
https://www.fontsquirrel.com/fonts/libre-baskerville
License — SIL Open Font License v.1.10:
http://scripts.sil.org/OFL

Vector graphics:

Tulip (recoloured and trimmed) from Art Nouveau Vectors by dumbmichael :
https://www.vecteezy.com/vector-art/193489-art-nouveau-vectors

Frames (recoloured) from DD Oval Vector Frames at http://www.vecteezy.com

Left silhouette (recoloured): from Silhouette Portraits by free vector: https://www.vecteezy.com/vector-art/75650-silhouette-portraits

ABOUT PAULA HARMON

At her first job interview, Paula Harmon answered the question 'where do you see yourself in 10 years' with 'writing', as opposed to 'progressing in your company.' She didn't get that job. She tried teaching and realised the one thing the world did not need was another bad teacher. Somehow or other she subsequently ended up as a civil servant and if you need to know a form number, she is your woman.

Her short stories include dragons, angst ridden teenagers, portals and civil servants (though not all in the same story — yet). Perhaps all the life experience was worth it in the end.

Paula is a Chichester University English graduate. She is married with two children and lives in Dorset. She is currently working on a thriller, a humorous murder mystery and something set in an alternative universe. She's wondering where the housework fairies are, because the house is a mess and she can't think why.

Website: www.paulaharmondownes.wordpress.com
Amazon author page: http://viewAuthor.at/PHAuthorpage
Goodreads: https://goodreads.com/paula_harmon
Twitter: https://twitter.com/PaulaHarmon789

Books by Paula Harmon

The Cluttering Discombobulator
Can everything be fixed with duct tape? Dad thinks
so. The story of one man's battle against common
sense and the family caught up in the chaos around
him.

Kindling
Is everything quite how it seems? Secrets and
mysteries, strangers and friends. Stories as varied and
changing as British skies.

The Advent Calendar
Christmas as it really is, not the way the hype says it
is (and sometimes how it might be) — stories for
midwinter.

Weird and Peculiar Tales (with Val Portelli)
Short stories from this world and beyond.

ABOUT LIZ HEDGECOCK

Liz Hedgecock grew up in London, England, did an English degree, and then took forever to start writing. After several years working in the National Health Service, some short stories crept into the world. A few even won prizes. Then the stories started to grow longer . . .

Now Liz travels between the nineteenth and twenty-first centuries, murdering people. To be fair, she does usually clean up after herself.

Liz's reimaginings of Sherlock Holmes, her Pippa Parker cozy mystery series, and *Bitesize*, a collection of flash fiction, are available in ebook and paperback.

Liz lives in Cheshire with her husband and two sons, and when she's not writing or child-wrangling you can usually find her reading, messing about on Twitter, or cooing over stuff in museums and art galleries. That's her story, anyway, and she's sticking to it.

Website/blog: http://lizhedgecock.wordpress.com
Facebook: http://www.facebook.com/lizhedgecockwrites
Twitter: http://twitter.com/lizhedgecock
Goodreads: https://www.goodreads.com/lizhedgecock

Books by Liz Hedgecock

Short stories
The Secret Notebook of Sherlock Holmes
Bitesize

Halloween Sherlock series (novelettes)
The Case of the Snow-White Lady
Sherlock Holmes and the Deathly Fog
The Case of the Curious Cabinet

Sherlock & Jack series (novellas)
A Jar Of Thursday
Something Blue
A Phoenix Rises

Mrs Hudson & Sherlock Holmes series (novels)
A House Of Mirrors
In Sherlock's Shadow (2019)

Pippa Parker Mysteries (novels)
Murder At The Playgroup
Murder In The Choir
A Fete Worse Than Death
Murder In The Meadow

Caster & Fleet Mysteries (with Paula Harmon)
The Case of the Black Tulips
The Case of the Runaway Client
The Case of the Deceased Clerk
The Case of the Masquerade Mob

Printed in Great Britain
by Amazon